It was the wedding invitation.

Megan picked it up, turned it over and read again. "Happy anniversary number twenty." Why was Alec showing her the card she had received at the café?

"This card was in the box that came to me," he said.

"Two cards?" Megan asked.

"Yes, two cards. The writing on the back of both of them appears to have been photocopied. They're identical."

"And you think there's a connection between these cards and the person who was shooting at us on the lake, plus the deaths of Sophia and Jennifer?"

He nodded. "There is no doubt in my mind. We're looking at someone from before..."

"From before what?" she asked.

"From before our lives now. It may be painful, but I think we're going to have to go back to the early days, when we were...together. Whoever is doing this is obviously from...then."

Books by Linda Hall

Love Inspired Suspense

Shadows in the Mirror
Shadows at the Window
Shadows on the River
*Storm Warning
*On Thin Ice

*Whisper Lake

LINDA HALL

When people ask award-winning author Linda Hall when it was that she got the "bug" for writing, she answers that she was probably born with a pencil in her hand. Linda has always loved reading and would read far into the night, way past when she was supposed to turn her lights out. She still enjoys reading and probably reads a novel a week.

She also loved to write, and drove her childhood friends crazy wanting to spend summer afternoons making up group stories. She's carried that love into adulthood with twelve novels.

Linda has been married for thirty-five years to a wonderful and supportive husband who reads everything she writes and who is always her first editor. The Halls have two children and four grandchildren.

Growing up in New Jersey, her love of the ocean was nurtured during many trips to the shore. When she's not writing, she and her husband enjoy sailing the St. John River system and the coast of Maine in their thirty-four-foot sailboat, *Mystery*.

Linda loves to hear from her readers and can be contacted at Linda@writerhall.com. She invites her readers to her Web site, which includes her blog and pictures of her sailboat, http://writerhall.com.

ON THIN ICE
LINDA HALL

Steeple
Hill®

Published by Steeple Hill Books™

STEEPLE HILL BOOKS

Steeple
Hill®

Recycling programs
for this product may
not exist in your area.

ISBN-13: 978-0-373-67409-1

ON THIN ICE

Copyright © 2010 by Linda Hall

www.SteepleHill.com

Printed in U.S.A.

Grace and peace to you from God our Father
and the Lord Jesus Christ.

—1 *Corinthians* 1:3

ONE

Her friends were dying and Megan Brooks knew she was next. She needed answers. And Alec Black, the sheriff of Whisper Lake Crossing, Maine, the man who had broken her heart twenty years ago, was the only person in the world who could give them to her. Yet she never imagined their meeting would be like this—the two of them standing face-to-face in the middle of a frozen Maine lake, ankle deep in snow.

People changed in twenty years. Certainly this man had. He was only nineteen when she had last seen him, and she a year younger. They had met when she was a camp counselor and he was a lifeguard at a summer Christian camp for kids. She had just graduated from high school and he had completed one year of college. Alec's brother had been in her high school class— and it was Bryan who had suggested that Megan and Alec meet in the first place. Even though Megan had dated Alec's brother briefly, he had seemed ecstatic when Alec and Megan fell in love.

All during the fall they saw each other. He was in his second year of college and she was in her first. They became inseparable.

By Christmas she was pregnant.

They decided to keep it a secret. They would get married immediately. Although the pregnancy was a mistake, they loved each other desperately. They were in love enough to make it work. Even though Alec's parents and the grandmother who raised Megan had wanted them to wait, they wouldn't listen. They planned their wedding for Valentine's Day. Megan's baby was due in July.

It was to be a small but lovely church wedding with only four friends in their wedding party. It was going to be perfect.

But the wedding never happened. All of that was twenty years ago.

Alec's eyes were the same—large and brown and expressive. However he now wore rimless glasses. The ends of his hair, which stuck out from under his knitted watch cap, were darker than she remembered. And his hair was now shorter. His hair was the first thing she had noticed about him when they'd met. In those days his hair hung long and sun-bleached in his eyes. She remembered the way he would brush it off his face with both hands.

From the first moment she saw him, she was aware of everything—the way her hair was, the way she looked in her one-piece swimsuit, self-conscious, knowing his eyes were on her from atop his lifeguard perch. And they were.

She wondered now if his hair would be as soft in her fingers as she remembered.

"Hello," he said uncertainly. "Pretty cold weather. You just out for a walk on the lake?"

He didn't know who she was. This was the sort of thing you would say to a stranger. She knew she had changed. In twenty years she had lost weight. "Pleasingly plump" was how her grandmother had described her back then. She had also exchanged the big, round, plastic glasses she wore for violet-tinted contact lenses. Plus she had cut her long "dirty-blond hair"—also a label from her grandmother—and now it was auburn in color and cheek length.

An attempt to remake herself? Possibly.

Flecks of snow landed on the shoulders of his bulky blue jacket. Up around his collar peeked a layer of red fleece. She fought the urge to reach up and straighten his collar.

"Hello." She looked directly into his eyes. Her voice was hoarse, a whisper. She needed to remember why she was here. This wasn't about them. This was about her friends. People had died. She could be next. So could he, for that matter. Unless he was the one responsible for the murders?

He peered at her, took off his glasses, folded them and put them in his pocket. He ran his hand over his face and squinted at her, then turned away. Then back at her. "Sorry," he said. "I just… You… For a moment…you looked like someone I used to know."

"I am someone you used to know."

She could see recognition dawn slowly. His eyes went wide and he took a step back, staring, not letting his eyes leave her. "Meggie?"

She nodded, winced slightly at his old pet name for her.

He came close to her, and she felt all the power of him again, a strength that had kept her rapt and spellbound twenty years before. Control. She needed to remain in control. It was twenty years later and she wouldn't be hurt again.

She said, "I came to see you. I need to talk with you."

"Meggie. You look so…"

"Different? I *am* different, Alec." She took a breath before she could continue. "I drove up yesterday. I got here last night. Someone at the sheriff's office told me it was your day off."

"You came…"

She nodded.

"After all this time…"

"Yes."

"How did you know where to find me?"

"A woman in your office said you like to ice fish on your day off. She told me where."

He ran a hand across his chin, still looking at her. "No, I mean Whisper Lake Crossing. How did you know I was here?"

"I looked you up online." Megan, who worked as a self-employed Web designer, had kept track of Alec over the years. She knew that he'd been the sheriff here for six years. She knew that he'd never married.

She continued, "I needed to come and see you because of Sophia Wilcox and Jennifer Moore. Do you remember them? From the wedding party?" She clamped her mouth shut. Had she really said the words wedding party? She had vowed she would not bring that up.

She shifted her position in the snow. Her toes were beginning to feel cold through her thin leather boots. "They died in separate car accidents last month. First, Sophia in California. Her brakes failed and she went down over a cliff into the Pacific Ocean. Then exactly a week later Jennifer died in Augusta. Here in Maine. Her brakes failed in precisely the same manner as Sophia's brakes and she went off an embankment to her death. I don't believe they were accidents…." She stopped, aware that she was now giving voice to her fears.

"Meggie." His voice seemed to have broken, or maybe it was the sudden gust of wind that had carried it from her. Seeing him in person was reawakening things in herself which had lain dormant for twenty years—things she had not allowed herself to feel. Why had she thought coming here would be a good idea? What could he do?

"I know all about those so-called accidents," he said. "You're right. I've been wondering about that very thing."

"I think I'm next," she said.

"You might be."

This startled her. She drew a breath and looked up at him. What did he know?

What happened next was so sudden it barely had time to register. His head jerked up. His eyebrows scrunched together as he looked at something beyond and behind her. Suddenly he reached forward, grabbed her shoulders with one arm and, with the other, he held her around the waist, brought her to him and dropped them both to the cold, snow-covered surface of the lake.

"Stay down," he said into her ear.

"Wha…?" she managed.

"Someone. With a gun. On the shore," he breathed. His mouth was close to her ear. He held her firmly.

It was then that she heard the sound of shots.

Minutes passed. Alec flattened himself against her and held his arm across her back. She felt the keen alertness in him. It was unbearable being this close to him.

More shots. Someone was after her! Someone knew she had come here! Long minutes passed, until finally, he crouched up beside her, his gun in his hand. "Stay down!" he hissed.

"Okay," she whispered. He didn't have to worry. She had no intention of getting up.

In the next minutes she felt or heard something that was like a thunder underneath them. In one horrific instant she thought the lake was cracking. She had visions of them escaping the shooter only to be plunged into the icy depths of Whisper Lake.

"The ice," she said. "It's breaking up!"

Alec brought his face close to hers and put a finger to her lips. "Shh. The ice is fine," he said. "It's just settling. It does that. It means nothing."

After several minutes of quiet, he got up but kept low. When she attempted to do the same, he cautioned her with his hand to stay down. She placed her gloved palms together and lay her face against the ice and watched him crouch toward the shore.

The cold and wet ice was seeping up her pant legs and inside her jacket and soon she was shivering, whether from cold or fear she didn't know. Probably fear. Someone had killed her friends and that same someone had followed her here! And she had no idea why.

It all had something to do with the card. As soon as she was handed that card when she had walked into the coffee shop this morning, she should have turned around and driven right back to her Baltimore home.

The shooting seemed to have stopped. She

looked up. Alec was scanning the shoreline, frowning. Megan rose to her knees. "Are you sure you saw someone?" she asked. "Maybe it was a car backfiring," she said.

He shook his head. "I saw someone. With a gun."

She shuddered.

His gaze seemed to settle on her for a long time. He pulled off his toque and gave it to her. "You need a hat. You're so cold, Meggie."

"I'm Megan," she whispered. "I go by Megan now." She pronounced it *Mee-gan*. She pulled Alec's toque firmly down around her ears. It was still warm from his head and it smelled like him.

There was a hint of a smile on his face. "Okay then, Megan…" He emphasized the name, elongating the *e*. "We have to get off this lake. Where's your car?"

"I parked it up by the town dock."

He said, "My stool and fishing gear are over there. I'm going to grab them and then we're going to make tracks toward your car."

"What about your car?"

"I live in town. I walked here."

The light snow had stopped and ice

crystals gave the air a sheen. As she walked in step with Alec, the events of the past two weeks came to her in sharp clarity.

Even though it had been a long time since the two had corresponded, it had been shock to learn that her school friend Sophia had died. She managed to find the e-mail address for Sophia's sister, Pam, and conveyed her sympathy. Pam was pleased to hear from Megan after all these years, but wrote back that the entire thing was "fishy." When the family was finally able to retrieve her car from the Pacific Ocean, they determined that the brake cables had been worn to the point of being nonexistent. This was so unlike Sophia, Pam wrote. Sophia always kept her things in pristine condition.

The police were looking into it, Pam had said. But they had no leads. Sophia left behind a husband and two children. Sophia was to have been maid of honor at Megan's wedding to Alec.

Seven days later when her other friend Jennifer had died in the same kind of accident in Augusta, Maine, Megan began to be afraid. Jennifer was to have been her bridesmaid.

"They've gone," he said. "Whoever it was."

"How do you know?" she asked.

"I saw someone get into a truck. We need to hurry, though." She kept in step with him. "Megan, do you have your keys?"

She pushed shaky, cold fingers into her pocket and handed him the keys to her Toyota. He could drive. She didn't think she would be quite capable.

"We've got to move," he said. "We're okay now. He's gone. But we've got to move fast. We have to get off the lake. We're sitting ducks out here."

She found it hard to keep up with his long strides. About a dozen feet from the shoreline she felt her feet slip out from under her. Before she fell, Alec reached one strong arm over and caught her. When they reached the shoreline, he was still holding on to her tightly.

All of this closeness to a man who had hurt her so profoundly was sending her very being into confusion. His touch was melting feelings long dead and cold within her.

"Alec, I have to ask you something.

Why did you leave?" she said as they reached the car.

He didn't turn to her and she wondered if he hadn't heard her. Perhaps not. Perhaps she only whispered it. She didn't repeat the question. But would she finally learn why he had walked away from her twenty years before?

TWO

Alec put the keys in the ignition of Meggie's silver Toyota and the engine came to life. He aimed it up toward the parking lot entrance. They needed to get out of there and he needed to figure out what was going on.

When they reached the street he pulled out his cell phone and made two calls in quick succession. The first was to his new deputy, Stu. "Someone is shooting out at the lake," he said. "About half a mile north of the fishing shacks. Could be kids." He knew it wasn't kids, but he was conscious of keeping his demeanor calm. He didn't want to show Meggie the rising panic he was beginning to feel. Megan, he corrected himself. "We need to check it out. Pick up any shell casings you can find. I'll be there as soon as I can…" He described the precise location and urged Stu to hurry. As best as he could remember he described the truck he'd seen leaving. "Dark in color. Late model, small. I wasn't close enough to get a make on it," he said.

He glanced over at Megan, and everything in him wanted to protect her this time, not leave her. Not like last time.

His next call was to his trusted friend, retired Special Forces Major Steve Baylor. Steve and his wife Nori owned and managed Trail's End Resort and Cabins. Alec often called upon Steve's expertise and Alec could sure use his friend's level-headed help right about now. Steve had worked more cases with snipers and ballistics and trajectories in a month than Alec had in his whole career.

"Steve," he said. "Someone's shooting out on the lake. I have a woman with me. We both were caught in the cross fire." For this call, Megan was just "a woman with him." He couldn't go into specific details on the phone. Even his closest friend, Steve, didn't know about Megan, about that part of his life.

Calls complete, he closed his cell phone and put it back in his pocket. He was glad he had insisted on driving. The woman beside him, who hugged her arms around herself, was in no shape to drive. Of course she was more than "just a woman," she was his Meggie. Even after all these years. He looked back at the road lest he let his gaze rest on her too long or spend too much time remembering and regretting.

Long-ago memories entered unbidden into his thinking as he drove. The girl he had fallen in love with had blond hair, which she wore straight and halfway down her back. Round glasses used to cover half her face. This Megan was thinner, more studious looking than his high school Meggie. His Meggie was pretty. This Megan, who folded her gloved hands on her lap to keep them from shaking, was stunningly beautiful. She still wore his hat. He liked the way it looked on her.

Alec already knew Sophia and Jennifer had died in car accidents. His brother Bryan, even from his home in New Mexico, kept track of everyone from those days. He'd called Alec with the news.

"They look to be too coincidental to me," Bryan had said. "Don't they to you?"

They did, indeed.

Megan shifted in her seat. He still couldn't believe that she was here in Whisper Lake Crossing. This time he would believe what she told him. This time he would listen to his own heart rather than the arguments and reasonings of his family.

He hadn't hung in there when Megan's grandmother had died and his own brother was arrested for the murder. But, more importantly, he hadn't believed Megan.

"Where are we going?" she asked.

"My office."

"Good. That's good." She looked down at her hands. "We need to figure this out." She paused. "I just want you to know that I never would have come if there was any other way. Just so you know."

She never would have come. Her words cut him to the quick. After his brother was arrested, he had tried to talk to her. He had called but she never answered. She hadn't even attended the trial. She had disappeared, and he was the only person who knew why she had left town in such a hurry. She had been pregnant, carrying his baby. It was a secret they had kept from everyone.

Their child would be almost twenty years old now. A grown-up person in his or her own right. Through the years he had thought of hiring a private investigator to find his child. He never did. He knew he didn't deserve to be the child's father. This was his penance for betraying Megan. He had done the only thing he could do in the ensuing years—he prayed daily for his child. He knew he had no right to ask, but another part of him reminded him that the baby had been his, too.

Megan pulled off his hat and laid it on her lap and sighed. She fingered a few loose threads and looked out the window. He drove past a few businesses, mostly closed up for the winter now. With temperatures hovering at twenty degrees below, few people were about.

Megan looked up, seemed to remember something, leaned forward and opened the glove compartment. She said, "This morning someone gave me this." She pulled a square white card out of a manila envelope.

He blinked at the large white rectangular card that Meggie held in her hands. The front of it was embossed in cherry blossoms and hearts. He recognized it immediately. It was one of their wedding invitations. She turned it over to show him the back. Written in large block letters were the words, *HAPPY ANNIVERSARY NUMBER TWENTY.* Their twentieth anniversary would have been on Valentine's Day. Valentine's Day was next week.

He skidded slightly on the slick road. "Who gave you that?" he asked, quickly regaining control of the wheel.

"This morning I went into a coffee shop and someone handed it to me. It had my name on it. Meg Brooks."

"What coffee shop?"

"The one with the big boat painted along the side."

He nodded. "The Schooner Café. Who gave that to you?"

She shrugged. "I don't know. I walked into the coffee shop and a waitress came over and asked me if I was Meg Brooks. When I said yes, she handed me this envelope. She said that someone had come in a few days ago with an envelope to give me when I showed up. When I looked at her in surprise, she said that everyone who comes to Whisper Lake Crossing eventually stops in there for coffee."

"Who knew you were coming here?" he asked.

"Nobody knew I was coming here." She placed the invitation on her lap.

Alec shook his head slowly. What was happening here? "Describe the waitress who gave that to you."

"She was blonde, big hair, sort of heavy, seemed talkative."

"That would be Marlene. She owns the Schooner Café."

He did a quick U-turn on the mostly deserted street.

"Where are we going?" she asked him.

"The Schooner," he said. "We need to talk to Marlene. We need to figure this out."

Megan nodded. "That's a good idea. Something weird is happening. I want to find out what."

They stopped at a red light. He looked

long and hard at her. He wanted to protect her. This time he didn't want to walk away from her. But this time would he be strong enough to stay?

THREE

Megan could tell he was watching her, studying her as they sat across from each other at the Schooner Café. He ordered coffees for the two of them, even though she didn't particularly want coffee. He hadn't asked her. He'd gone ahead and ordered. Their waitress was a pretty, dark-haired, tall young woman whom Alec seemed to know.

"My mother's just at the bank for a minute," the girl said in answer to Alec's question. She poured coffee into two white mugs and set them down on the table between them. "Would you like something to eat? Would you like menus?"

Megan shook her head and encircled the cup of coffee with her hands. It warmed them.

Alec added, "No. We just need to see your mother."

"She should be back in a minute. You want me to call her on my cell phone?"

"If you wouldn't mind," Alec said.

Megan looked down into her coffee, stared into the swirling brown liquid.

She couldn't meet Alec's eyes. She was afraid of what he might ultimately ask.

She had left because of their baby. Her pregnancy was beginning to show and she vowed then that no one would ever know she was carrying Alec's baby. She was young, unmarried and ashamed. When he left her, when he didn't believe her, she meant to take their baby away from him forever.

She pretended to study the saltshaker. Alec took out a small notebook and began writing something down in it. For a long time they sat there thinking their own thoughts and not talking.

A few moments later the door opened and in breezed the blonde woman who had given the envelope to her this morning. She came over to their table and shrugged out of her bulky pink faux fur coat.

"Selena said you wanted to see me, Alec? Oh, hello," she said to Megan.

"We meet again," Megan said quietly.

"Yes. It's nice to see you." To Alec she said, "Selena said this was important." There was concern in Marlene's blue eye-shadowed eyes.

"It's about this envelope." He showed her. "Do you know who gave this to you?"

Marlene shook her head. "I have no idea. I've never seen the man before in my life. He came in here and said that when Meg Brooks showed up to please give her this. Then he handed the envelope to me. I said, 'I have no idea who Meg Brooks is.' And he said that in a few days a woman would be coming in here, a stranger, and I was to ask her name and give her this letter." She looked at Megan. "I figured it was something you were expecting."

Megan was about to say something, and Alec said, "What did he look like?"

Marlene sighed, her eyebrows furrowing. "Well, let me think. I would say he was about your height, Alec. Give or take.

Medium build. Really dark hair. I remember that. Black and thick."

"Beard? Clean shaven?"

"I don't remember a beard. So, probably clean shaven. I like a beard on a man. I would have remembered a beard."

"Dark complexion?"

"I really don't remember. Not black. But not swarthy."

"Didn't you think the whole thing was kind of odd?"

"I thought it was odd to begin with, but after a while I really didn't give it much thought. I figured Meg Brooks must be a relative or something." Marlene crossed her arms over her sizable bosom and nodded. "Is this important?"

"It might be. Did he say where he was staying in town?"

"I got the impression that he wasn't staying anywhere in town, that he was just passing through."

"What gave you that impression?"

"I don't know. Just the way he seemed, all in a hurry or something. And he seemed nice enough, so I took the envelope and

said, 'I can't promise anything, but sure.'
Then this morning Meg Brooks in the flesh
shows up." She looked down at Megan.

"Did this black-haired man tell you what
Meg Brooks was supposed to look like?"

Marlene shook her head. "That's the
strange part. When I asked him this, he just
shook his head and said that I would know
her when I saw her and how many people
come into Whisper Lake Crossing in the
middle of winter anyway."

"That's what he said?"

"Right."

"Why didn't you call me?" Alec asked.

"Call you about what?"

"And you didn't think this whole thing
was strange?"

"I thought it was plenty strange, but a lot
of plenty strange things happen around here
and I don't go to the sheriff's office with
every little strange thing, Alec. This just
seemed an innocent thing. Someone
dropping off a letter for someone who
would be coming by later."

"When did this happen?"

"Let me think." She put her hand to her

forehead. "The day before last. Yes. That's what it was. In the morning."

Alec scribbled something in his book. He looked up. "Marlene, if that guy comes back, please contact me immediately."

"Okay." Marlene saluted him. If the situation hadn't been so grave, Megan would have laughed out loud.

Later at the sheriff's office, Megan was formally introduced to his office assistant, Denise, who was the woman Megan had spoken to earlier. She was a middle-aged, comfortable-looking woman.

"Stu got your call, Alec. What's going on?" Denise asked.

"Some maniac was out there on the lake shooting."

Denise looked from one to the other. Without explaining who Megan was, Alec ushered her past two yellow chairs in the waiting room and into his office.

Denise called after him. "Your mail's on your desk, Alec."

"Thanks," he said as he closed the door behind them.

His was a modest square office, very efficient, very plain. It had one desk and two chairs. There were few touches of home. No family photos that she could see. On the wall was a picture of a sailboat. He pushed the small stack of mail aside and offered Megan a chair.

At the bottom of his stack of mail there was a shoe box, which was wrapped in brown paper. Something about it seemed to pique his interest. He pulled it out from the stack and looked at it. It seemed to be secured all around with thick layers of packing tape.

He turned it over, examined it, dropped it on the desk, and for the second time that day he lunged for Megan and said, "Out! Now!"

He opened his door, ushered her through it quickly, calling to Denise as he did so.

"Anyone else in the building?"

"Alec, what's up?"

"We have to get everyone out now. I think somebody just sent us a bomb!"

Ten minutes later, Megan found herself two blocks from the sheriff's office, sitting on a damask-covered, spindly chair in

Denise's kitchen, surrounded by bobble-heads and dolls.

"Here," Denise said. "Let me move these dolls at least. I collect them, make and sew clothes for them. I'm getting ready for a show. But they get a bit over-whelming at times."

Megan barely heard. She had no choice but to sit here and drink Denise's burnt instant coffee and think about the fact that somebody wanted her dead.

When Alec finally arrived, his expression was grim. Both women looked at him expectantly.

"It wasn't a bomb," he said.

"Well, thank the good Lord for that!" Denise placed a hand on her chest.

"Yes. We can be thankful for that," he said.

"What was it, then?" Megan asked.

Instead of answering, he said, "Denise, may I speak with Megan alone? Can we use your parlor?"

"Certainly, Alec. Would you like coffee? We were just enjoying a cup."

"Thanks Denise. That would be great."

Sill unsmiling, Alec led Megan into a

small, windowed room which, like the kitchen, was entirely populated with dolls. A bald-headed doll sneered and bobbed toward her as they entered.

Alec plucked two cloth dolls with pinched faces from a chair and sat down. She sat in the chair opposite him. She turned the grinning bobblehead away. Something about it made her uncomfortable. As she did this, Alec piped up, "I see you've met Denise's dolls."

"There are sure a lot of them."

They both smiled a bit. Obviously, Alec had said this to lighten the mood. It didn't last long.

"If it wasn't a bomb, then what was it?" Megan asked.

From inside his jacket he took out a clear plastic bag and laid it on the coffee table next to a china doll with pink round circles for cheeks. It was the wedding invitation. She picked up the plastic bag, turned it over and read again. *HAPPY ANNIVERSARY NUMBER TWENTY.* Why was he showing her the card she had received at the café? She already knew this card all too well.

"This card was in the box that came to me."

"Two cards?" she asked.

"Yes, two cards. The writing on the back of both of them appears to have been photocopied. They're identical. We're sending them both to the forensics lab."

"And you think there's a connection between these cards and the person who was shooting at us on the lake, plus the deaths of Sophia and Jennifer?"

He nodded. "There is no doubt in my mind."

She shuddered and pulled her sweater tightly around her.

Alec took a notebook and pen out of his breast pocket and began to write. He was quiet for a few minutes. The only sound was the rhythmic clanging of a clock on the mantel. Megan's mouth felt dry.

He looked at her for a few more moments and then asked, "Where is it that you live now?"

"Baltimore."

"What do you do there?"

"I'm a Web designer." He wrote the answers carefully in his coil-bound notebook. She knew his handwriting; his tall, compact letters. She had received love letters in that careful script. She had gotten rid of all of them. Back when she had burned her wedding dress and ribbons and decorations and candles, those love letters were in the same pile.

"Do you work for a company?"

"Alec, are you questioning me? Interrogating me?"

A look of surprise crossed his face. "Yes, Megan. I want to get to the bottom of this." He smiled at her.

This bothered her and she didn't know why. She looked away and felt slightly insulted. She was not some suspect. She was personally involved in the case. She found herself retreating from his gentle smile.

He was a cop, trained to get information and confessions from suspects by any means possible. If that meant cops had to pretend to have feelings they didn't possess, they would. And for the briefest of moments she'd actually thought he was showing her kindness. She needed to be on her guard.

"I'm not at fault," she said, sitting stiffly

in her chair. "Something is happening to me and I'm not the cause of it."

His voice was soft. "I never said you were. I'm just trying to get a handle on things. This is the only way I know how to work, by asking questions." He put his pen down. "I'm sure you've thought about this. Do you know of anyone who might want to do this to you? Maybe from your work?"

"I have dozens of clients, most of whom I've never even met."

He raised his eyebrows.

"That's the way I work, Alec. I am alone."

"I can't imagine you working in a job that doesn't include people…."

"I told you. I've changed. I could ask you the same question. Is there anyone *you* know who would want to do this to us? Besides, why would one of my clients target you? I've never told anyone about you. No one knows my history."

He took a breath and looked down at his notebook. If her words stung, that's what she wanted.

She sighed. This was getting them no-where. "In answer to your question." She paused. "After the trial I went to Baltimore to live with my godmother, a close friend and college roommate of my mother's. Her name is Eunice Schneider. She came into my life after my grandmother died. She offered a place for me to stay in Baltimore. I went. I had no place else to go. She was good to me. I went to school there, took a graphic design course. For the past ten years I've been designing Web sites. I do okay for myself. I lead a quiet life."

He said, "So, we're looking at someone from before…"

"From before what?" she asked.

"From before our lives now. It may be painful, but I think we're going to have to go back to the early days, when we were…together. Whoever is doing this is obviously from…then."

She could tell it was hard for him to say the words, but she too realized it had to be someone from those days. Isn't that why she had come here? After she had gone over and over Sophia's and Jennifer's deaths in her mind, had spent many sleepless nights in Baltimore wondering if she might be the next target, she had decided to come and talk to Alec.

"Someone from before," she said. "I don't know where to begin."

"We begin at the beginning."

"Right."

He was looking at her, his expression so tender, so questioning. She knew. She knew that he wanted to ask about their child.

And she wasn't ready to tell him about that. Not yet.

FOUR

It was late afternoon by the time Alec arrived home. He had told Megan that he would keep in touch and let her know what forensics found out about the invitations and if they found anything out on the lake.

Every time he had looked at her, something inside of him went to pieces and he completely forgot all police procedure, everything he had ever learned.

He tried to concentrate on the case. He remembered Sophia Wilcox as a short, pudgy, flighty, dark-haired girl. Megan and Sophia had been friends since kindergarten. His brother Bryan had dated Sophia briefly. Then again, his brother Bryan seemed to have gone out with everyone briefly.

He went on to the police database and

looked through the report on Sophia's accident. Her car had gone over an embankment on a highway in California and had tumbled down a cliff into the sea. There wasn't much left of the car and driver, but bits and pieces seemed to indicate that the brakes had been seriously worn down. She left behind a husband and two children.

He turned to the report about Jennifer. Once upon a time, before he met Megan he'd had a crush on Jennifer. However once he met Megan, he judged all other women by her. Jennifer had wanted to be a missionary he remembered. She planned to go to Africa or China. She always said that as soon as she graduated from high school she would leave Augusta, leave Maine for good.

But out of all their friends, she was the one who stayed in Augusta. Jennifer had died in precisely the same manner as Sophia had. She had drowned when her car went over a hill into a reservoir near her home in Augusta. She left behind a husband and three children.

Alec looked at his watch and decided that with the time difference, it wasn't too late to call California. When he was put through to the officer investigating Sophia's death, he identified himself and asked if there was any new information on the car accident.

It took a while for the detective to even find the case report on his computer or in his files. Finally he said, "We've put that death down to an accident. We are thinking that maybe she simply fell asleep."

"The report said the brakes failed."

"The brakes were not good. But the car was so destroyed we couldn't know for certain," the officer said.

"Anything about the crash strike you as strange?" Alec asked.

"The family insisted that she had had her car in for a service that very day."

"You talk to the mechanic?" Alec questioned.

"Yes. He said the car was in good working order when she drove it out of the shop. He checked the brakes and they were fine. Just curious. What's your interest in all this?"

Alec said, "A second person died the same way here in Maine. Her brakes failed. The two were friends." He told the officer about the wedding that didn't happen. He omitted the fact that he was to have been the groom.

"That's interesting. Maybe this case deserves a second look," the officer said.

"I guess it does," Alec said.

They exchanged names, numbers and e-mail addresses. They promised to keep in touch. It was a start.

It was probably too late to call Augusta, but Alec did anyway. He found Detective Brantley Peterson, the officer who had handled Jennifer's case, still in his office working.

Alec identified himself and told him the same story he had told the officer in California.

"Things have happened here," Alec said. "Another member from that wedding party came to see me today. She's worried for her life."

"Why'd she come to see you?"

"She's an old friend. She received a copy of the invitation from that twenty-year-old wedding," Alec answered.

"Did the other women receive the invitation prior to their deaths?"

"I don't know, but it would be worth checking into."

"Yes, it would."

When he hung up, he realized how difficult it was going to be to keep his connection to Sophia, Jennifer and Megan a secret. It was only a matter of time before someone found out. He was handling the whole thing very badly. He needed to be honest. He needed to pray.

He couldn't pray for himself, but he could pray again for his child, and he could pray for Megan. He prayed for her safety. He prayed for wisdom for himself and Steve, and for everyone working on this case, but he didn't—couldn't—pray that he and Meggie would find their way back to each other. That would require too much of him. He would have to repent the one secret sin that had been a part of his life for twenty years.

Before he closed his laptop, he saw that he had a new email. The subject line read: MEGGIE.

He stared at it. She had sent him an e-mail?

He clicked on it. The e-mail wasn't from Meggie. He stared at it in growing horror.

THE SHOOTING WAS A WARNING. NEXT
TIME I WON'T MISS.

He read the e-mail again and again. The
sender was an innocuous Web e-mail
address that was simply a series of
numbers. Maybe Adam, his favorite geek
from the church youth group, could tell
him exactly where the e-mail came from.
Stu had some expertise on the Internet,
but sixteen-year-old Adam seemed to
know everything there was about e-mail
and the Internet.

He forwarded the whole message to Stu
and then e-mailed Adam. He also decided
to head over to Steve's to get his take on
things. He printed the e-mail.

But getting Steve involved at this level
would mean sharing a part of him that no
one knew about.

Alec wondered if it was worth the risk.

Nori Baylor, the proprietor of Trail's End
Resort, where Megan had rented a cabin,
had invited Megan and the other cabin
guests up to the lodge for coffee and dessert

that evening. Nori's daughters and her husband Steve were going to be there.

The lodge was brightly lit when Megan got there. As she walked up the shoveled path, various motion lights lit her way. Now that she knew that Steve, who used to be a police officer and sometimes worked with Alec on cases, was the owner of the place, she felt immediately safer.

Nori was at the front door to the lodge even before Megan had a chance to knock. Nori said, "Come in, come in. You're the first to arrive." She opened the door wide. "My daughters are here, but Steve isn't back yet." Nori's smile was happy and bright. Her eyes sparkled. Megan wondered what it would be like to be so content. And so in love.

Inside, Megan hung her jacket on an ornate coat tree by the door. She commented on it and learned it was an antique that had been unearthed from a big room of treasures behind the kitchen.

Megan was led into the main living room, which was huge and high ceilinged. Nori had set out small silver bowls of candy and nuts and the place smelled of apples and cinnamon.

"I've got some mulled apple cider on the go," Nori said. "Have a seat in here and I'll be right in. Daphne, Rachel, come meet our guest."

A moment later Nori's daughters entered. Megan had been told they were twins, yet obviously they weren't identical. The one who introduced herself as Daphne was taller and seemed a bit more outgoing. They shyly said hello and then scurried off to help their mother in the kitchen. Megan sat on a brown leather couch and gazed at the roaring fire.

Nori entered with a tray, set it down on the coffee table and sat down across from her. "I'm so glad you could come up this evening," Nori said. "I don't know where the other guests are, but I'm sure you'll meet them. Vicky and Brad are their names. Also, Steve should be along soon, too. He had to go out with Alec for a minute—" Nori stopped and put a hand to her mouth. "I'm sorry to bring that up. I forgot."

Earlier in the afternoon when Nori had

come to Megan's cabin to give her more towels, Megan had told Nori about what happened on the lake, leaving out the part that she and Alec knew each other. The story she had told had her out for a walk on the ice, and just happened to run into the sheriff, and that shots were fired out on the lake.

Nori touched Megan's arm. "I'm so sorry this had to happen to you."

"It's okay."

"So tell me about yourself," she said. "You're from Baltimore?"

Megan nodded.

"What do you do there?"

"I'm in graphic design."

"Graphic design! I'm an artist, too."

"Really, well, I can't call myself an artist. Not anymore so much. I mostly manipulate computer images. I haven't done any creative stuff for myself in a long time. Not since I studied it in school."

"My late husband taught fine arts at a university…."

And they were off and running, talking about art. Megan learned that it was Nori who had painted the big mural of a schooner on the side of the Schooner Café.

"Later," Nori said, "I'll take you up to my loft and show you some of my works. One of the things I would really love to do here is to have a retreat for artists. That was my goal when I bought this place. We wanted to make it a retreat center for Christian artists, writers and musicians. So far it's just a guest resort—and that's fine—but our future plans call for more retreats."

"That sounds like a wonderful idea." Megan found herself warming to Nori. Maybe she would even go to an artists' retreat.

A few moments later there was the sound of talking and stomping of boots at the kitchen door. Megan looked toward the kitchen. Alec was entering with a big man. He was as tall as Alec, but bigger all-around. She presumed this was Steve.

Alec saw her and stopped in his tracks. "Hello," he said.

"Hi." Nori waved a few fingers at him and smiled.

Nori said, "I would introduce you, but I know you met earlier on the ice."

"We did," Megan said, smiling sweetly at Alec.

He kept staring at her. Finally he asked, "What are you doing here?"

It was an odd question and Nori laughed lightly. "Alec, she's staying here in the cabin called Grace."

Grace was the largest of the Trail's End cabins that Nori had shown Megan. The cabin was the farthest from the lodge but the closest to the road. All the cabins used to be numbered and they were just referred to by their numbers, but Nori and Steve had given each cabin a name.

"I don't know why, but I got the idea you were staying in town," Alec said to Megan.

"I thought this was town."

Alec's eyes locked on to Megan's and hers to his. They were like this for several seconds until she picked up her cider and brought it to her lips. Nori broke the silence by saying, "What a horrific thing to happen to a guest. You arrive on a bit of vacation, you decide to go for a walk on the ice and the next thing you know someone is out there target practicing." To Alec she said, "I was just thinking it's a good thing that you were out ice fishing. What a wonderful co-incidence. I might even say that God may have been at work there…."

Megan nearly choked on her cider.

Steve said, "We're taking the shooting very seriously. We don't think it was just people randomly target practicing."

"You don't?" Nori's eyes were wide. She looked at Alec. Obviously she thought the gunman was after Alec, maybe for a past crime he had solved or someone he had successfully put into prison. "Oh, Alec, that's awful," Nori said. "Are you able to stick around for a while or do you have to get back to work?"

"We're back to work," Steve said. "We're checking on a threatening e-mail."

Nori nodded. "You guys don't need to stay. You go and take care of that e-mail. We can't have this kind of crime around here."

Megan asked, "Is there anything you need me for?"

It was Steve who answered her. "Not

really. Not now. Alec said you didn't see anything. Is that right?"

Megan said she hadn't.

"The less we need to involve you the better," Steve said.

Megan raised her eyebrows and stared hard at Alec. Imperceptibly, he shrugged. Obviously, he hadn't told Steve about their previous relationship.

Later, after she got back to her cabin, all she felt was regret and a kind of deep sadness. It was as if she was being hurt all over again. She would bury herself in her work this evening, and try not to think about a boy from twenty years ago who had ridden her on the handlebars of his bicycle, down the hill while she laughed and yelled at him to go faster, faster, faster.

When she checked her e-mail, the message with the subject line, OUR HOUSE, barely registered. Since she got a lot of spam, she deleted the e-mail.

And then she didn't know why—something about the subject line caught her attention—she retrieved the message from the trash folder.

The message simply read, WE WILL BE
TOGETHER SOON. OUR HOUSE IS
ALMOST READY. Attached was a photograph of a house. Normally she didn't open
strange attachments, but this one displayed
automatically when she opened the e-mail.
She studied the photo. The house looked
vaguely familiar. Or maybe it was that tree
in front of the house which she thought she
recognized. Or did she?

Several hours later, she woke up. She had
been dreaming about her son. Megan got up
and sat at her little kitchen table and opened
up her laptop. She looked at the picture of
the house and read the e-mail again.
Suddenly she realized that she knew that
house. It was the house she lived in until
she was five and her parents had died. The
tree was the little sapling she and her father
had planted so long ago. In the picture the
tree had grown, the trunk thick and strong,
the branches dense, profuse with the rich
green of late summer.

This house, this tree was just an hour
outside of Augusta in a town called Bath,
Maine. When her parents died, she had

moved in with her grandmother who lived in Augusta. In all the years she had lived in Augusta, she had never gone back to look at the house in Bath.

WE WILL BE TOGETHER SOON. OUR HOUSE IS ALMOST READY.

What did this mean? That she was going to die next? That soon she would be joining her parents? Did this whole thing have something to do with *them?*

FIVE

Megan read the message again, studied the picture, looked at the e-mail address from which it was sent. The address was a series of numbers and letters.

She needed Alec on this. He was her only connection with the past. Even though it would be painful, they had to work together on this. She had come this far after all.

She called him.

"Alec here." His voice was gravelly with sleep.

She looked at her watch. Maybe six-thirty was a bit early in the morning. "Did I wake you?" she asked.

"Who is this?"

How could he not know her voice? "It's Megan."

"Oh…Meggie…Megan. Oh."

He seemed flustered.

She said, "I got an e-mail last night…"

A pause. "About the shooting?"

"No."

"Megan?"

She held the receiver tightly to her ear. "It was a short, cryptic e-mail with an attachment. It was a picture of a house. Alec, it's the house in Bath that I lived in until I was five. I recognize it!"

He said, "We should meet. We need to talk. About a lot of things. I've spoken with the investigating officers regarding the accidents in California and Augusta. Plus…I got an e-mail, too."

"The same one?"

"Not exactly. I'll show it to you. As much as Steve thinks we should keep you out of everything, you probably should know about this."

She paused before asking, "Steve doesn't know about us, does he?"

"No," he said evenly. "Not yet. We should talk. We need to talk this through."

"I agree," she said.

"How about one hour? The Schooner Café for breakfast. I'll see you there."

"I'll be there."

"Can you forward me the e-mail and picture?"

She did.

When she got to the Schooner Café an hour later, it was busy. Alec, however, wasn't there. She checked her watch. He was five minutes late. Not a lot. People could be five minutes late and nothing might be wrong. Then why did she feel so nervous? She scooted into a booth and a horrible déjà vu settled over her. Maybe he wouldn't come. Maybe it would be like last time.

Marlene came over with the coffeepot and said, "Megan! I didn't see you there in that booth or I would've come over sooner. I have a message from Alec. He was here around half an hour ago working on his computer and then he left. I think he got a phone message or something. He wants you to come over to the sheriff's office and wait for him there. He shouldn't be more than half an hour. He said it's important, an emergency."

"Did he tell you what the emergency was?" Megan asked, sliding back out of the booth.

"No, he didn't. Could you wait for a minute? I was just in the middle of making a breakfast sandwich for him when he had to leave. Can you take it to him, if you wouldn't mind?"

Megan said she would and also ordered a muffin and coffee to go for herself.

Since the sheriff's office was just a block away from the Schooner Café, Megan decided to leave her car where it was and walk. She passed a small drugstore with an elaborate Valentine's Day display in the window. She had to turn away.

A couple was walking toward her, arm in arm, up the cold, slippery street. The woman was slightly taller than the man was. She was skinny with long, straight hair down to her waist. This looked like the couple who was staying in a cabin down from her own at Trail's End. The woman's long hair swayed from side to side as she held on to the man's arm and laughed. The woman looked a little older than Megan. A streak of pure white ran from her left temple and down through the length of her long hair.

The man was big, had white hair and a gray beard. He was jolly looking and wore sunglasses. Megan had seen this man last night when she had looked out of her cabin window. There was something about him even then which gave her a momentary pause. But this morning he looked like a harmless Santa Claus.

They struck her as a comfortable married couple on a little winter vacation. Megan looked back at the Valentine's Day display and was suddenly envious. She wondered what it would have been like to have been married to Alec for twenty years.

As the couple made their way past her, the man nodded slightly in her direction. There was that feeling again. It was something she couldn't put her finger on. When he caught her staring at him, and raised his eyebrows above his sunglasses, she quickly looked away.

Megan arrived at the sheriff's office and Denise ushered her in to see Alec. His lips were pressed tightly together in a thin line.

She set his coffee and bag of food on his desk. While she waited for him to speak, she sat down and unwrapped a muffin.

On his desk was a printout of the e-mail she had received and a color copy of the house picture.

"You got my e-mail, I see," she said.

He nodded. "And this is the one I received." He pushed a piece of paper across the desk at her. She read it.

"The shooting was a warning? A warning about what?" she asked.

He shook his head. "I don't know." Abruptly he said, "There's been another death."

"What?"

"Do you remember Paul Magill?"

She felt a shiver of fear. He was to be Alec's groomsman. "How did he die?"

"Same as the other two. The brakes on his car failed. He hit a truck."

"Where did it happen?"

"He lived in Augusta. It happened last night. My parents called me this morning."

"Had you kept in touch with Paul?"

Alec shook his head. "A little. Not with Sophia and Jennifer, of course, but I kept in touch with Paul and…"

Bryan. She looked up at him but didn't finish his sentence. She didn't mention the name of the brother who by his horrific actions had effectively stopped their wedding and driven them apart.

Megan didn't move. She put down her muffin and wiped her fingers on a napkin. "How is he?" Megan asked drily.

Alec looked up at her sharply. "I told you he's dead."

Megan put the napkin on the table. "I didn't mean him. I meant…Bryan."

"Good. He's good." Alec felt his hands stiffen at his side.

"Is he still in…?"

"Prison?" He finished the sentence for her. "No. He's been out almost ten years now."

"You're in touch with him then? He lives nearby?"

Alec shook his head. "He doesn't live near here. He moved to New Mexico when he was released."

"New Mexico. Why did he move so far away?"

"He wanted to start over."

"Well." Megan looked around the room but didn't finish her sentence.

Bryan was the little brother he had protected against all the bullies of the world, and he was still doing it. Because of his father's failing health, his parents couldn't make the trip to see their youngest son anymore, so Alec had taken over that responsibility. Alec said, "He works at an electronics store."

"He was always good at that sort of thing."

"He's a Christian now. He accepted Christ in prison."

Megan nodded.

Five years into his sentence, Bryan had eagerly told Alec that he had found God through a prison Bible study. God had changed him. Correction—He was changing him. It was an ongoing process that God was helping him through, he told his older brother.

Alec continued, "He still goes to church where he lives. He has a girlfriend. My father can't fly, so Bryan and Lorena, his girlfriend, are saving up money to fly out here to get married."

"It's weird," she said. "That a person can kill someone and go to jail, and then just come out and lead a normal life like nothing happened."

He looked down at his desk, at the two e-mails side by side. He lined up their edges. "It hasn't been all that normal. He's been through a lot of counseling. He's prayed and paid his debt."

"My grandmother is still dead."

He looked into her eyes. "I'm sorry, Megan. I shouldn't have said that. Nothing will make up for the death of your grandmother, I know that." He paused. "I never got a chance to tell you how sorry I was then."

She said rather thoughtfully, "The confusing thing is that Bryan was someone that I liked. Used to like."

Alec agreed. "We all used to like him. He had his problems but he was genuinely likable." Megan had even dated Bryan a few times. But when Bryan introduced Megan to Alec that summer at camp, it was the end of anything between Bryan and Megan. Bryan had understood when Alec and Megan got together. He'd laughed about it, actually, made jokes about how his older brother had "stolen his girlfriend." "The best man won," Bryan had said, playfully punching his brother in the shoulder. They were all still friends.

"Sophia used to have a crush on him," Megan said.

"A lot of girls did."

"He was a bit of a rebel, but people liked him."

Yes. Bryan was a likable guy. That's why it had made no sense at the time that Bryan would deliberately push Megan's grandmother down the stairs to her death. No one could believe that Bryan would actually do that. There was no cause for it. They all got along. Megan and Alec were going to have a big happy family wedding.

And then Meggie had found her grandmother at the bottom of the basement stairs, her neck crushed. She died in the hospital two days later from a massive head wound but not before she told everyone, including the police, the EMT attendants, and Meggie herself, that it was Bryan who had pushed her down the stairs.

The accusation was ridiculous, of course. Everyone knew that Megan's grandmother was in the early stages of Alzheimer's. Yet the forensic evidence proved otherwise. They found evidence of Bryan's presence at the scene of the crime all over the place—hairs on her body, his skin under her nails, evidence of the struggle. In addition, Bryan had a gash on his right cheek made by her fingernails.

To top it off, a witness, a neighbor, said she'd seen Bryan and Megan's grand-mother arguing several times. This witness said under oath that the young man had shoved the woman very roughly in the driveway not two days before her death. As to why he would push Megan's grand-mother or what they were arguing about so strenuously remained a mystery to this day.

"Are you worried Bryan is next?" Megan asked.

Alec looked at her. That was exactly what he was worried about.

She looked away. "I can't do all this. Our son is dead. I've had enough pain," she said.

His head jerked up at her. He wasn't sure he had heard her correctly. "Megan?" he said tremulously.

"Our son was stillborn. There was a heart defect. He never had a chance. I thought you should know."

It felt like a punch, as if someone had hit him hard in the gut expelling all of his air. There just didn't seem to be enough air in the room for him to find another breath. *You never told me,* he wanted to yell at her. *Why didn't you tell me? Why couldn't I know this?*

"What…happened?" he asked.

"I went to live with my godmother in Baltimore and it happened there. The baby was a boy. In my mind I've always called him Jack. After my father."

He said, "There was nothing the doctors could do?"

Megan shook her head.

"Megan." He looked into her eyes where a tear welled in her left eye and another wandered down her cheek. She brushed angrily at them with her fists. He wanted to go to her, hold her in his arms and never let her go.

I've had enough pain. That's what she had said. She had lost her parents, his own brother had killed her grandmother and her son had died.

"Megan," he said. "I'm so very sorry."

How could he have done what he did to her? Oh Megan, Megan will you ever forgive me for putting my family, my brother, ahead of you and the love we had?

SIX

His son had died.

For twenty years he had prayed daily for a child who didn't exist. But was what she did in not telling him any worse than what he did? Because when all the craziness happened, he had chosen his brother, his family, over Megan.

Alec remembered when his brother had come home on the night her grandmother died. He had been agitated, full of wild energy. He couldn't settle down and kept running his left hand over a scratch on his cheek.

Alec had demanded, "What did you do to yourself? What happened?"

"Nothing. It's nothing. I fell. Let's go shoot some pool."

"I'm going to Meggie's."

"No. No you're not. You can't. Not now. You're going to come with me." He grabbed Alec quite roughly and Alec shook off his grasp. "What's the matter with you?"

Alec began to be afraid. This was the old Bryan. The angry Bryan, not the likable Bryan he showed to the world. This was the Bryan who would go stomping through the house shoving his foot through the wall. This was the Bryan who his parents couldn't control, the Bryan his mother cried over. He decided to go with Bryan that night. He needed to placate him. If Bryan's old demons were back, Alec needed to protect him. But even with these outbursts, no one could quite believe that Bryan would hurt an elderly woman, would actually commit murder. In the ensuing years Alec had wondered at his mother's denial, his father's preoccupation when it happened.

It fell on Alec, the oldest brother to protect the youngest son. No one told him to do this, not his parents, not his teachers, it was just something he took on himself.

And he still did.

The following morning he'd learned that Megan's grandmother was in the hospital. She had fallen down the basement steps and broken her neck. She died on Valentine's Day, the day he and Megan were to be married.

After Megan left his office, Alec sat at his quiet desk with the door closed and put a hand to his forehead to quell the pain that was starting there. He lifted up the receiver and punched in Bryan's cell phone number.

"Bryan? This is Alec."

"Hey, bro. What's happening?"

"Paul's dead."

"Tell me you're kidding. Please say you're making this up." Was there a hint of fear in Bryan's voice? "How do you know?" Bryan asked.

"Mom and Dad called me this morning and told me."

"Oh man."

"The brakes on his car failed."

A silence. "So, just like the others."

"Yes. Just like the others."

Alec held the receiver to his ear and looked at the e-mail messages still lying side by side on his desk. "I'm calling because I want you to be careful."

A bit of a chuckle from his brother. "Don't worry, bro, I'm pretty safe here. I'm not likely to go driving a car anytime soon. I never got my driver's license after getting out. I don't trust myself at the wheel."

"Just watch your back."

"Lorena does the driving for the two of us."

"That's good. Have you gotten any strange e-mails lately?"

"E-mails? None that I can really think of. You want me to go back and look in my trash folder?"

"I would, yes. And let me know. Mom and Dad would want you to be careful."

"Don't worry. If I feel in peril, I'll just rob a bank. That'll land me in jail. I'll be safe in there."

"Don't joke, Bry. This is serious."

Bryan promised he would be careful.

Afterward Alec felt heartened by the call. Bryan sounded good. Maybe things would get better. Maybe church was good for him. Maybe Lorena was good for him.

Yet always, always, there was that sliver

of fear when he hung up from talking to his brother that things were not as good as Bryan made them out to be. He knew he needed to go out and see him. It had been a while. He needed to make sure his brother was okay.

She had always blamed her sins for her aloneness in this world. A Christian girl getting pregnant when she was eighteen was bad. She knew better. She'd been raised by a good church-going grandmother yet she had slept with her boyfriend. Just once. And had gotten pregnant. No wonder God was judging her.

When she first feared that she might be pregnant, Alec was the first person she told. They sat quietly on the park bench when she told him. The town was all decorated for Christmas. In the distance there were carolers.

She'd been surprised at his reaction. Instead of being upset or even afraid, he'd been pleased. He'd smiled. His dark eyes sparkled. Then he laughed. He had clasped his hands around her waist and danced them around the snow in the park.

Megan looked out of her kitchen window to distract herself from those thoughts. A woman was making her way toward Megan's cabin now, over the mounds of snow and rocks and roots in the back behind the cabin. The lights of a cabin glowed behind her like squares of bright yellow against the black sky.

When Megan opened the cabin door, the woman said, "I thought I would come and introduce myself."

This was the woman she'd seen that morning with her husband in town.

"Hello," Megan said. "It's good to finally meet you."

The woman wore a red plaid coat and a striped knitted hat with pom-poms. The whole outfit was rather endearing. She held the length of her brown hair with one hand to keep it from swirling around her face in the wind. She had broad cheeks and a generous smile.

"I'm Vicky." The white streak in her hair didn't make her look older, it made her look charming.

"Nice to meet you. I'm Megan."

"I arrived the other day. I'll be here a week," Vicky said.

"I think I saw you this morning in town with your husband."

Vicky laughed out loud, a boisterous sound, and leaned her head back. It was almost, but not quite a cackle. "My husband? We just met. That's Brad. He's in the cabin beside mine. Even though he's a bit older than me, we seemed to really hit it off. I've always liked older men."

"Wow."

"He's just such a big sweetie. You heard about the storm coming next week? I'm wondering if I should leave now or wait until the deluge of snow is over. It's supposed to be one low-pressure system after another for a while. And that means snow, snow, snow. How long are you staying?"

Megan said she hadn't given much thought to the storm, but that her stay depended on how long her business would take.

"Business," Vicky said, and stuck out her tongue. "Me, no business for me. I'm on the rebound from a bad relationship and needed some time away. That's why

I'm here. Trying to get centered. I saw a catalogue with this place listed, so I phoned. Voilà! I'm here, and what a beautiful place.

"I'm sure this will be good for me. I've never done anything quite so spur of the moment before, coming to a cabin like this by myself. And then meeting a nice guy right off the bat. Brad and I had dinner last night at his place. I was over there introducing myself and then before you know it, he's panfrying trout and eggs. We were going to head up to the lodge last night but we never quite made it." Her eyes twinkled and Megan thought that it didn't take Vicky too long to become interested in someone else after coming off a bad relationship.

"You want to come over? Brad wants to meet you."

"Me? Now?"

"A little while ago, he said to me, 'Have you met the woman in the farthest cabin over? What's she like? We should get together all three of us,' and so I thought, since it's just the three of us here right now, why don't you come on over to my cabin now. Brad's cooking up shrimp with his special shrimp sauce."

Megan thought about it. Maybe it would be nice to get her mind off everything for a while. "I can bring crackers and cheese," she said. "Let me just finish off my e-mail."

"You people with your e-mail. Brad's the same way. Always with his laptop, day and night. Me? I don't even have a computer. Don't have TV either. Just me and my animals and my organic garden. Who goes on vacation and brings their computer?"

She came into Megan's cabin and said, "Wow, you certainly got the deluxe model. I don't even have a fireplace. Just a bitty woodstove. This is beautiful."

"Yes. It is nice." Megan had booked the most expensive cabin because she wanted a separate bedroom. Some of the cabins were little more than one room.

"Brad's is like this too," Vicky said. "Brad is a documentary filmmaker. He's doing a documentary on the lake. You should see all the gear he has. Cameras, that sort of thing."

On the way to Vicky's cabin, she said, "Nori said you design Web sites."

Megan said she did.

"Well, between you and me, I think it's the Web site thing that has Brad interested in meeting you. He told me he's in the market for a new Web site for his film company."

When they got to Brad's cabin, he called out, "Come on in, you two beautiful ladies." When Megan approached, he took one of her hands in both of his. "So nice to meet you." Even though they were inside, he wore his sunglasses.

Megan watched Vicky fuss with the fire and Brad panfry shrimp on the woodstove in a big cast-iron frying pan. Brad was a heavy man with wild hair and a shaggy gray beard, a bit of a crooked nose. But, what Megan noticed were his large white teeth which seemed to protrude a bit oddly and crookedly from his mouth when he laughed. Which was often. She wasn't surprised that Vicky was attracted to this mountain man. He seemed nice and could cook, obviously. He wore a plaid cotton shirt and jeans and moccasins.

The little cabin smelled wondrously of garlic and butter and Megan found herself relaxing. Almost.

A kettle on the woodstove was whistling and Brad said, "I'm making tea for you ladies."

The three of them stood around the steamy kitchen rich with aromas and drank tea and ate shrimp. At one point Vicky nudged Brad, "Tell her about your monster film."

"Monster film?" Megan put her tea on the counter.

"He's working on a film about the Whisper Lake monster."

"I didn't know there was a Whisper Lake monster."

Brad leaned forward, grinning with all his teeth and said, "Yep."

"So where does he go when the lake is frozen?" Megan asked.

For a moment his face darkened. "Well, I guess that's the question, isn't it?"

Megan felt an instantaneous flutter of disquiet which dissipated as quickly as it had come.

"Yeah, Brad," Vicky said. "That's what I keep asking. Wouldn't it make more sense to come here when the lake *isn't* frozen?"

Megan could hear the wind outside high

in the trees. "I plan to," he said quietly. "This is just the beginning. Just the beginning, ladies."

After her second cup of tea and more shrimp, Megan felt satisfied. She was tired, yet Brad talked on and on. Vicky had drawn her knees up and seemed content to listen to Brad's exploits. He'd been to the top of Mount Robson in Canada. He'd been bungee jumping in South Africa and done a film about clock-makers in Germany. After a full recounting of his African safari, Megan was dying to get back to her cabin and her comfortable bed and away from this man who now seemed pompous and self-absorbed her. She couldn't understand how Vicky could hang on his every word. When there was a lull in the conversation, Megan yawned and said, "Well, I think I should be getting back to my place. I'm dead tired."

"No." The way Brad said it so quickly took both women by surprise.

He said, "I've done all the talking here tonight, we haven't let our guest introduce herself properly. Where's home for you, sugar?"

Sugar? "I live a little south of here."

"Where's a little south of here?"

"Oh, here and there. I'm from here and there." Megan looked past him toward the window. She was feeling more and more uncomfortable, yet it was nothing she could name or her put her finger on.

Vicky playfully punched him again. "If our guest doesn't want to tell us where she's from, then that's her business. Look at me, I didn't want to tell anyone about my life but you got it all out of me." Her giggle was a cackle.

He leaned over and kissed Vicky on the cheek. "But I want to know where a lovely young woman like Megan lives. I'm good with accents. That's one of my interests," he said.

She didn't want to tell them where she was from. She didn't want anyone to know she was here. She didn't want to put anyone in danger.

Brad leaned toward her again and she could see his eyes through the dark glasses. It was as if she had looked at those eyes in a dream. She drew back.

"I hear you do Web sites," he said.

She hugged her knees and yawned again. "We can talk about that sometime."

He said, "Do you have a card or something?"

"A business card? Not on me."

Vicky stood up and grabbed a piece of paper and a pen and handed it to Megan saying, "Please write down your information for Brad so we don't have to talk business anymore."

Megan wrote her Web site on the paper and handed it to him. He peered down at it, seemed satisfied, folded up the paper and put it in his pocket.

As Megan was putting on her coat, Brad said, "You know what day it is next week?"

The women shook their heads.

"Valentine's Day. Women like you two should have sweeties to keep them warm I should think." Megan stared hard at him, but he abruptly changed the subject. "You happen to know where I can rent a snowmobile around this place?"

Megan shook her head. "Maybe someone in town would know."

Brad said, "Maybe the sheriff would know. I'll contact the sheriff about it. Have you met him? Alec. Is that his name?"

There was something in his eyes when he said the word *sheriff,* almost a half wink.

"I have to be going," she said. "I have to get back."

Her hands trembled as she zipped up her jacket, and on her way back to her cabin, she thought about what he had said. The sheriff. What did Brad want with the sheriff? Why was he looking at her that way when he talked about the sheriff? And why did that request make her feel so uneasy?

SEVEN

At quarter after nine the next morning, Megan saw Alec's car drive up the road and past her cabin and toward the lodge. She stepped into her boots and stood on the back stoop of the cabin as she watched him park near the lodge. He made his way not up the wide steps to the lodge door, but to another cabin close by. A brown dog bounded out to meet him and Alec bent down and scruffed him around his head.

She hated to admit it, but she loved the sight of him.

After she had escaped from the clutches of Brad and Vicky last night, she had sat at her laptop and done some online searching. She read again the accounts of the deaths of Sophia, Jennifer and Paul. Who was doing this? She wondered. None of it made any sense.

All night she had gone over lists in her head; old school friends, people who liked her, people who didn't like her, current clients, former clients. But if someone wanted to kill the wedding party, then why wait twenty years? Her head hurt from all the thinking.

She grabbed her jacket and put it on. She decided to walk up to the cabin that she had seen Alec enter. The snow that had been threatening last night had turned itself inside out and the morning shone with sun. It was even a bit warmer. She stepped into the felt-lined boots that Nori had loaned her, which belonged to one of her daughters. As clunky and big as they were, they kept her feet warm. She trudged up the cleared pathway. She didn't see either Brad or Vicky. Good.

She knocked on the cabin door. Alec opened it. He seemed surprised to see her. She entered the warm room. A brown dog bounded playfully at her feet.

"That's Chester," Alec said with a grin. "Steve's dog."

"Where's Steve?"

"I don't know. I came here looking for him. I'm heading up to the lodge next."

She bent down and patted the top of Chester's head.

"I told Steve about us," Alec said.

"That's good. I guess."

"He has some interesting ideas."

"Really?"

Alec said, "Come for a walk with me. I want you to see something."

He wanted to go for a walk? "Okay."

"I also want to talk to you about something."

"Okay."

They took off up what looked like a snowmobile trail. It was plowed and easy to navigate. The path became steeper and more slippery as it went farther into the woods.

They had climbed up the trail and were at a cleared place which overlooked the lake. It was gorgeous, full of sun in the early morning.

"This is what I wanted to show you," he said. His smile was shy. He wanted to show her this? Why? She asked him that.

"Because this is such a great view."

She wondered if he was thinking about the first time they had hiked a path together. The two of them had climbed Mount Katahdin in Maine with a group from camp. That day was the day they fell in love. That was the day he had kissed her for the first time. As they stood together now, she found herself softening. Had he taken her up here so she would remember? Why did being with this man confuse her so much?

Down below them on the lake, Brad and Vicky were snowshoeing. She could almost hear their laughter way up here.

"My cabin neighbors," Megan said. "Interesting people. I had shrimp and tea with them last night."

"Shrimp and tea. Interesting combination."

"It is."

"That's them?" He pointed.

"Yep."

"The guy looks sort of familiar."

"That's what I thought. But I think it's just because he looks like every picture of Santa Claus we've ever seen."

Alec shook his head as if trying to loosen an annoying thought. "I wanted to tell you about Steve's good suggestions," he said.

"Suggestions about what?"

"He thinks we should get a copy of your class yearbook. Sophia and Jennifer were in your class. And Bryan, too."

"Paul was a year older, and you were two years older."

"Still," he said. "A lot of our friends would be in that yearbook. Steve also suggested going through our old guest list for the wedding. Obviously someone kept their invitation."

"Someone had two of them. Do you even remember who we invited?"

She was conscious that they were standing very close together.

He said, "Not exactly, but I'm sure between the two of us we could come up with a pretty good list. Do you have your high school yearbook? We could piece things together from it."

Megan shook her head. "I honestly have no idea where my yearbook is. Maybe when I moved to Baltimore I left it at my grandmother's house. I was confused then. I didn't take a lot of my stuff."

He nodded, a faraway look on his face as he gazed past her down to the lake to where Vicky and Brad were slowly maneuvering through the snow. Vicky punched Brad playfully in the arm. He reached down, grabbed a handful of snow and showered her with it. Megan could hear them laugh from here.

"Did you tell Steve about my grandmother?" Megan asked.

"I told him as much as I thought he needed to know."

"Right."

"So I didn't tell him about your grandmother," he said. "Nor about my brother."

"So you didn't tell him everything?"

"I suppose I didn't."

"That's probably good." She took a breath and continued, "All I want is to know why someone plans to kill me. I don't know how going through an old yearbook and rehashing things will help anything."

"It might jog a few memories, things

we've forgotten, people we don't remember. Names. Faces." He paused. She waited.

Alec said, "My parents might have a yearbook. There might be something at their house." They were making their way back down the hill. In the short time they'd been walking, the sun had disappeared and clouds were moving in.

He continued, "When my brother was sentenced to prison, my mother boxed up all of his stuff. I bet there's a yearbook in there. I was thinking of going to Augusta for a few days, see what I can find. I also want to talk to Paul Magill's family. And the police there, too."

Megan said, "I'll go with you."

Alec stopped on the trail and looked down at her. "You want to go with me?"

Megan thought about it. "I do. And if there's time I'd like to drive by my old house in Bath. See if it's like the picture."

"Are you sure you want to come?" he asked.

"Yes. This whole thing is about me as much as it's about you."

"I was planning on staying overnight."

"Fine, I'll get a hotel."

"My parents have a big house. I'm sure you can stay overnight there."

"Okay. I'll stay with them," Megan said quickly. And then she thought about it. Staying with his parents? When they were engaged, Alec's mother had been so kind to her that Megan began to wonder if his mother could be like a mother to her.

But then they seemed to side with Bryan. Against her. Or at least, that's how it felt at the time.

She said, "Are you sure your mother would like to see me? Much less have me in her house?"

"My mother would love to see you. She often talks about you."

Megan raised her eyebrows at that. They were stopped in the path and stood underneath the snow-covered branches of a cedar. It was like their own private cave. "All of us," he said, "my family, me, have done a lot of thinking about things since…everything happened."

"What kind of things?" She looked at him expectantly.

He sighed. "A lot of things. Bryan has changed. God has changed him. If you had a chance to meet him you would see that. But back then, my mother would never admit that Bryan had problems. She's never been very strong. But we, none of us, thought that he could actually kill anyone. I guess we've never understood why he would do it. That's the big thing, the why. Your grandmother was such a nice person. Everyone loved her. I thought Bryan did, too."

As Alec talked about the woman who had raised her, Megan felt tears form. He went on, "But he's paid for it. Ten years in prison. We're all trying to give him another chance."

Megan thought about that. Would she ever be able to forgive the man who had pushed her grandmother to her death? In her own strength, she didn't think so, but maybe with God helping her, she could. She asked, "Does he come home very often?"

Brad and Vicky's laughter wafted up the mountainside.

"I try to visit him from time to time. But he still feels lost and humiliated, I think. There are so many things here he has to live down. He just doesn't think people here will ever accept him the way he is now, changed. They'll still remember the bully Bryan, the angry Bryan, the Bryan who could possibly murder."

"Do your parents fly out and visit him?"

Alec shook his head. A small clump of snow fell from the tree and landed on his cheek. He brushed it away. "My father can't fly. I've offered to take my mother with me, but she doesn't want to leave my father. So, she's waiting for Bryan to finally find it within himself to come home."

"Maybe with his fiancée?"

"That's what we're hoping."

Megan looked down at the expanse of frozen lake.

"Then tell your mother I'm coming, too. I'd like to visit her. I'd like to be a part of this investigation."

"Can you leave today?" he asked.

"Today?" She raised her eyebrows.

"I want to get there and back before the storm hits. I'll call my parents, tell then you're here and that you're coming. My mother will like that."

I hope so, she thought. He took her arm and headed back down the trail. Could she forgive Bryan? Could she forgive his parents? Could she forgive Alec for not standing by her? Maybe meeting his parents was a start toward a life of forgiveness, a life of grace, a life of peace.

Brad and Vicky were heading right toward them on the path, but when they saw Megan and Alec, Brad took Vicky's arm and steered her abruptly away and down another path. It appeared to Megan to be deliberate. She looked at Alec sharply, wondering if he noticed that too, but he seemed to be lost in his own thoughts. She was about to say something, but then decided that she didn't need to trouble him with the strange behavior of her neighbors. But, down at her cabin she was still troubled by it.

Megan sat quietly in the passenger seat of Alec's car as they made their way out of town that afternoon. How strange, he thought, sitting so close to her yet having so much time and space between them.

They were not the same people as they

were years ago. And he wondered if they had any future at all together. This crime would be solved, whether by him or by other police officers, and then she would be on her way back to her home and her life in Baltimore.

How he wished that things could have been different. How he wished he hadn't messed up so badly back then. And now they were on their way to see his parents. Back when they were engaged, his mother had really liked Megan.

"You have chosen a wonderful girl to marry," she had said. "Even though your father and I weren't sure you were ready for a step such as marriage, we're both quite taken with her. I think we're all going to have a long and wonderful relationship."

"Do you go back a lot?" Megan suddenly asked him.

He didn't immediately know what she was referring to, back here? He said, "I visit my parents about once a month."

"How's your mother? You said she was frail."

He shrugged. "You'll see her. Things have been hard for her."

Megan turned to look out at the snow-covered scenery scuttling past them. After a while she said, "I've never been back. Just before the trial I left. I never wanted to return." She blew out a breath. "What's our schedule?" she asked him.

"We'll head to my parents' house first. My mother's expecting us for supper. She was so pleased when I called her this morning and said you were coming. Tomorrow I have to go to the police station to talk with investigators there. I also want to talk to Paul Magill's parents. After that we'll drive by your house in Bath and then head back to Whisper Lake Crossing."

"Can I go with you to all those places?"

"I don't know if you'll want to."

"Of course I want to. This concerns me. We're in this together."

He glanced over at her, at the determined to set of her mouth.

"Yes, we are, aren't we?" he said. He hoped it was true now. He wondered if the two of them had a second chance.

They were quiet for the next few minutes. He wondered what she was thinking.

"Did the police have a chance to look at the invitations yet?" she asked.

They were still being examined in the forensics lab, he told her, but preliminary examinations for both of the invitations revealed that the box and the invitations were free of any kind of fingerprint evidence. Probably whoever had packaged up the invitations wore gloves. Stu had again questioned Marlene and her daughter, Selena, and other patrons in the restaurant that morning, trying to determine the identity of the black-haired man who had dropped off the envelope for Megan. So far they'd had no luck.

Alec continued, "Tonight we'll have a look at the yearbook, go over our guest list and try to think about who might want to harm us."

"People with grudges from the past. I can't think of any."

"Neither can I."

He also told her that they had carefully searched the grounds where he'd seen the truck and they could find no gun shells. "I've even had a team out on the lake. Steve's been out there. We can't find anything."

She said, "So whoever it was went out and cleaned up after himself."

"It would seem so."

She stared straight ahead.

Just outside of Bangor, Megan's cell phone chirped. She looked down at it. "That's my ring for a text message." She played with a few buttons. "My neighbor at Trail's End wants me to do his Web site, but…" She paused. "I don't know how he got my cell phone number. Wait." She looked up at him. "I guess I gave it to Nori and Steve. Maybe that's how he got it." She appeared to be thinking. "I wrote down my contact information for him, but just my Web site and the name I use as a designer."

"What do you mean the name you use?"

"I don't use the name Megan Brooks on my Web site."

"Why not?"

"I guess after everything that happened, I just wanted to be anonymous."

Alec thought about that. "Now I know why I wasn't able to find you on the Internet."

"You were trying to find me?"

"When this happened, yes." Which was

a lie. He had been trying to find her for a very long time before that, but on his own. He was afraid that if he looked too much and too hard, he might find her. And he couldn't risk that. Not after what he'd done.

"Oh."

After another period of silence, he said, "Megan…when you told me about your… about our son…you said you were in pain, or that you have had enough pain."

"That's right."

"I just wanted to say…I want to apologize. I'm sorry that I wasn't there when… he was born. That I wasn't there for you. It must've been a difficult time."

"It was," she said sharply.

"It was wrong of me. I should've been there. And I wasn't. I was stupid back then," he said. He shook his head. "I lost the best thing that ever happened to me."

She surprised him by saying, "We were both stupid. I should've let you know about the baby. It's partly my fault."

"Megan, you have nothing to apologize for."

They were at the outskirts of Augusta

now. She turned to him. "Why did you become a police officer? I don't remember you being interested in that."

Her question surprised him. He said, "Back then I wanted to be a teacher."

She smiled shyly. "I remember that."

"I guess with everything that happened to Bryan, I wanted to, I don't know, make things right, somehow." He shook his head. "Can't explain it." As he drove down the road leading to his parents' house he realized that he hadn't shared this precise reason with anyone before.

"And you never married?"

He shook his head. "I never did."

"No one took your fancy?" She gave him a sideways glance.

They were at a red light. He looked over at her. He didn't remember her eyes being that brilliant blue. It disturbed him that he had forgotten something so basic about her. No. There was no one in twenty years who remotely came close to being as special as she was.

Yet the closer they came to his parents' home, the more he could feel her tense beside him. The fingers of her right hand actually trembled as she drew her hair away from her forehead.

He looked back at the road and frowned.

Because there was still a little piece of the Bryan puzzle that he hadn't shared with her, something only Bryan knew, yet something so awful that he doubted whether Megan, or anyone could forgive him.

"Megan?" He turned. "Are you going to be okay?"

"I don't know." She fidgeted with her fingers. "I really don't know if I can handle everything that's happening."

The small firs on Alec's parents' property were bigger and fuller than Megan remembered. The house itself seemed a lighter color or maybe it was the addition of shiny, brown shutters that made it look so different. She hadn't remembered shutters. Alec pulled in behind a gray compact car in the carport.

Since the front walkway was drifted in with snow, they went around to the back. Alec led the way through the carport and she followed half a step behind him. So many memories flooded over her. Could she really be back here? Would she actually see his parents in a few moments? She tried to keep her knees from buckling underneath her.

As they got to the back of the carport, Megan's breath caught. A long time ago Alec had leaned her up against this very wall. He had taken her face in his hands and kissed her in a kiss that went on and on. She looked at him now and wondered if he remembered that at all.

"Don't be afraid," he told her.

"I'm not." She smiled. "Well, I guess I am a little."

When they arrived at the door, the first face that Megan saw when it opened belonged to Alec's mother. Dorothy Black used to be a slim, pretty woman with softly waving blond hair. The woman who greeted them at the door was birdlike thin. Her hair was now white and fine and caught up along the sides in bobby pins.

She wore a ruffled apron that went up around her neck and tied in the back. Her thin fingers fluttered by her sides. She seemed extraordinarily nervous, but maybe having Megan show up without much notice would do that to a person.

As Megan made her way into the once familiar kitchen, she could barely keep her knees from wobbling. It was only Alec's hand on her arm that kept her moving forward.

Behind Alec's mother stood his father. Mr. Black had gained considerable weight, and leaned heavily and awkwardly on two canes. After his mother gave Alec a hug, she turned to Megan. "Megan, it's nice to see you again."

"It's nice to see you, too, Mrs. Black." She shifted her gaze. "Mr. Black."

Mrs. Black pressed her hands together and said, "Come here, then."

Megan did so. The woman hugged her and Megan could feel the bones protruding in her shoulders. When the hug ended, she said, "How about we dispense with the Mrs. Black. Call me Dorothy."

The last time Megan had seen this woman was two days before her grandmother died. Dorothy had come over with some antique china that had belonged to Alec's grandmother. Dorothy wanted Megan and Alec to have it.

"You're going to be the next Mrs. Black," she had said. "So this belongs to you."

It was a set of delicate china, pale blue flowers on a white background. Megan had no idea where all of those plates and dishes and teacups had ended up. With the help of her godmother, she had left the house in the hands of a lawyer who put the contents up for auction. Maybe Dorothy came over and collected it all again. By that time Megan hadn't cared.

Alec's dad extended one hand and Megan shook it, then gave him a quick hug. "Call me Charles," he said. She smiled and said she would. Despite everything that had happened, it was good to see these two again.

"I need to get things ready in the kitchen," Dorothy said. "You three sit in the living room and catch up." Dorothy's eyes darted from one to the other and back again.

The living room looked only marginally different from the one Megan remembered. There was still the overstuffed floral furniture, the La-Z-Boy, the wooden rocking chair that Alec's grandfather had made, the hassock, the fussy lamps on end tables.

But the television in the pine cabinet had been replaced by a large flat screen mounted on the wall.

As well, the wall-to-wall beige carpet had been replaced by fringed, rose area rugs. The floors beneath them were now burnished oak. It looked nice, and Megan commented on it. The fireplace mantel was still covered with china ballerinas interspersed with framed photos of Alec and Bryan as young boys. These hadn't changed at all. Perhaps when Dorothy came into this room, she wanted to be reminded of happier times, a time when one of their sons hadn't been in jail.

Megan studied the boyhood photo of Bryan and felt a pang. She had lost a son, too. She and Alec had kept her pregnancy a secret so at least she didn't have to explain to his parents why there was no baby. Through the open door she could hear the rattling of pans and spoons and pots.

There was only one newer picture and Megan noted it. It was Alec decked out in his full police uniform. It looked like some very official event—maybe his graduation.

When the three of them were seated, Charles leaned over and whispered to Alec, "Too bad about Paul. What's going on there, do you know, son? And Jennifer, too. We used to see that girl from time to time in the mall." He shook his head and made a tsking sound. And then in a voice barely audible, he said, "Your mother's worried about Bryan."

"That's why we're here," Alec said.

"Have you spoken to your brother?"

"I did. He's okay. I told him to be careful."

Charles patted Alec's knee. "Your mother gets so upset about all of this. It plays on her and she worries."

"You okay in there, Mom?" Alec called. "You need a hand with anything? It smells delicious."

"It sure does," Megan agreed.

She carried a wooden spoon into the doorway and waved it. "I'm fine. You three just sit. You know me, I like to get things ready on my own."

In no time at all, the four of them were seated around the large dining table, which was covered with a gaudy flowered lace tablecloth. It looked to be set with the best dishes, although not the ones that Dorothy had given Megan. The whole evening began to feel surreal to Megan. She barely spoke as she looked from one face to another. The food was wonderful, and there was plenty of it, but Megan hardly tasted it.

During dinner, Megan got another text from Brad. She'd set her phone to vibrate and, trying to be as inconspicuous as possible, she took it from her pocket.

Hey, he wrote. You're not in your cabin. Worried about you. Thought we could get together this evening re. the Web site.

As surreptitiously as she could she wrote, We'll talk tomorrow, late.

She sent it and then switched off her cell. "Sorry," she said to Charles who was eyeing her across the table. "Business."

Outside somewhere, a siren whined. Wind blew against the house. The candles in the middle of the table flickered.

"Oh dear," commented Dorothy. "I hope we don't lose power."

Charles said, "Big storm coming next week. We'll all have to be hunkered down by then."

Over dessert, Dorothy said, "I put the box of old school stuff up in your old bedroom, Alec." Then to Megan she said, "I've made up the guest room off the kitchen for you, dear."

"Thank you."

After they ate, Charles took Alec down into the basement to look at some new tools he'd gotten and Megan went to the kitchen and tried to make conversation with Dorothy as she carried things from the dining room to the kitchen on a tray.

"It's so nice to see you after all this time," Dorothy said again, fidgeting and darting her eyes. "When Alec called this morning and said you were back, well, I just couldn't believe it. I raced around. Got a roast out of the freezer."

"You didn't have to go to any trouble," Megan said.

"It's no trouble. It's nice to see you again. It's nice to see that you both took the time to come down here for a little visit."

"We're actually here because of Jennifer and Sophia and Paul." As soon as she said it, Megan wished she could take back the words.

The blood looked to have drained from Dorothy's face. She took a moment to lean against the kitchen counter, and put a hand to her head. Then she fiddled with the bobby pins in her hair. "Terrible car accidents, weren't they?"

"I'm so sorry, Dorothy. I guess I shouldn't have brought this up. I know this must be hard for you."

Dorothy swallowed several times and put a hand to her throat. Her face was drawn. A vein in her forehead pulsed.

Megan scooped the rest of the mashed potatoes into a plastic container to put into the refrigerator.

And suddenly stopped.

Attached to the fridge by a magnet was a color picture of a slender blonde woman. The woman was standing next to a palm tree. Her hair curled softly on her shoulders. She wore a green sheath dress that came to her knees. Megan thought she knew this woman. She was sure of it. She unhooked it from the magnet and studied it.

"Who is this?" Megan asked.

"That's Lorena, Bryan's girlfriend. He e-mailed us that picture of her some time ago."

The woman in the photo had a full pouty mouth. It was as if she was telling the world that she was unhappy and didn't want to be here. "I know her," Megan said.

"You do? She lives out somewhere in New Mexico. She and Bryan go to the same church. Have you been out there? Have you met her?"

Megan stared at the picture and shook her head. No, she had never met Lorena but she knew this woman all the same. She didn't know how she knew Lorena. She just did.

A water glass slipped from Dorothy's hand, and it shattered on floor. "Oh no. Oh my goodness, my clumsiness."

Megan tacked the picture back onto the fridge and found a dustpan and brush. "Here, let me help you," Megan said gently.

As she bent to clean up, she was sure she saw tears in the older woman's eyes.

When she looked back at the picture on the fridge, she didn't know what it was, but the picture seemed "off" somehow and she couldn't figure out why.

EIGHT

"I know that girl," Megan told Alec later after Dorothy and Charles had gone to bed, and she and Alec were sitting in the kitchen going through the yearbook. All evening long she had thought about the girl whose picture was tacked up on the refrigerator. She kept glancing up at the girl.

"You've been through every picture in the yearbook," Alec said. "And you haven't found anyone who looks remotely like her. They say everyone has a double. Maybe she only looks like someone you think you know."

For the past hour they had gone through Bryan's yearbook. They were looking for anyone who stood out, anyone who had threatened either of them back then. Even as a joke. From the yearbook they were also constructing a guest list. Alec's laptop was open on the kitchen table and name by name, he was running them through his various police search engines to see if anyone had a criminal record. It was a place to start.

"Maybe this whole thing has been a waste of time," Megan said.

Alec shook his head. They were sitting across from each other at the kitchen table and he looked tired. He ran a hand through his hair and sighed. "It's not a waste of time. Don't say that, Megan. It was good for you to come. I am enjoying being with you."

Her heart fluttered. Megan looked at him for a long time. *He was?*

"Plus it was good for you to see my parents again. I worry about my mother."

"She seems nervous. She dropped a glass in here. I'm afraid it was me who made her nervous. I mentioned the car accidents and perhaps I shouldn't have."

Alec said, "My father told me she's finding it more and more difficult to face reality. She's always been like this to an extent. Growing up, I had to take care of her a lot. I still do. She only wants to hear the good about Bryan. None of the bad."

"I thought there was nothing bad about Bryan now."

He paused before answering. "He still has his challenges at times."

Maybe it was because she was overly tired, but her voice almost snapped when she said, "I thought everything was just great with him."

Alec eyes darkened for a second. "Sometimes people don't want to take a chance with an ex-con. He's had a bit of trouble keeping a steady job."

Megan stared at him.

Alec said quietly, "My parents don't know this, but I've loaned Bryan money from time to time."

"Really?" Why were alarm bells going off in her head?

"He's my brother. Someone has to take care of him." Alec went back to the computer and Megan flipped through the yearbook again, her thoughts tumbling around her. She said, "As soon as we find out who's doing this, as soon as the cops find the killer, I'll be going back to Baltimore. You won't need to worry about me anymore."

"Megan, don't say that. I don't want you to go."

She gazed at him for several minutes, her heart melting. Was he being truthful with her, or would he just leave her again? She got up, turned her back to him and dug through the box filled with pictures, trophies, notebooks, artwork.

Also on the table was Alec's computer. As they went over the names on the wedding guest list, he would search for them online. But as much as they tried, they couldn't come up with any names of anyone who would want to kill Sophia and Jennifer and Paul.

Even though she'd been through it moments before, she sat back down at the far end of the table and opened up the yearbook again to the first page. And as she wandered through the book again, she realized that this was Bryan's yearbook. All of the autograph signatures were made out to him. She ran her fingers over the pictures of Sophia and Jennifer. They had signed his yearbook and written messages to him.

Megan and Bryan had dated briefly in May before they decided they would be friends only. Bryan was funny, but at times too much an actor. Often she didn't know if it was the real Bryan talking or someone he was trying to emulate. He was funny, but she wanted someone real.

Sophia had written, "Happy Bry! The happiest guy in the world. Let's always be free and happy like we are today!"

Happy and free. Megan sighed deeply.

Alec said, "Anything jumping out at you?"

She shook her head and yawned. She looked at Bryan's senior picture. He was a member of the computer club and the radio control model club, she noted.

"I've been looking up the guest list names online and I'm coming up with a few names that I'll e-mail to Steve," he said. "There are a few kids I can't find. I also found three who have small criminal records."

"Really? Who?"

"Someone named Jeffrey Brown. You remember him?"

"Jeff Brown? Maybe. Wasn't he Bryan's friend?"

"I think. He's got a couple of DUIs. And he lives in Wyoming. Still, it's worth checking. I'll get his name to Steve."

"Who are the other two?"

"Meredith Tarlton and Daniel Besthedder."

She shook her head. "I barely remember them."

"Daniel was involved in a hit-and-run and Meredith was involved in a drug bust."

Megan went to the back of the yearbook and looked up the three names. Jeff Brown was a junior the year Megan, Bryan, Sophia and Jennifer graduated. Was it significant? She went to his picture, but couldn't remember him at all. He'd written something to Bryan though. "Let's stay in touch, buddy."

Meredith Tarlton was dark haired and Goth-like with black-outlined eyes. Megan only remembered her peripherally. She hadn't autographed her picture to Bryan.

She turned to Daniel's picture and remembered him. He had worked on the yearbook with her, but he was a junior when she was a senior. He had written, *Here's my best to you and Megan. I hope you have a very happy life together.*

Obviously, not everyone knew that Megan and Bryan had decided to be just friends.

She flipped through to the back of the book reading notes and signatures. On the inside of the back cover she read something that made her pause. *Megan will always be mine.*

She pushed the yearbook across the table to Alec and pointed. "This is Bryan's yearbook. Why would he write that?"

For several minutes Alec looked at the writing. He finally said, "I know Bryan's handwriting and that's not his."

"So, whose then?"

"I don't know."

After Megan retired to the guest room and closed the door, Alec put the yearbook under his arm, turned off the light and headed upstairs to his boyhood bedroom.

Even though the hour was late, he didn't sleep. He knew he wouldn't. He often didn't when he stayed here. It had to do with this place, this room. Too many memories. Mostly about his brother, and not all of them good. For about a year he'd shared this room with his brother until Bryan's antics got out of control and they needed to keep them separate. From the beginning Alec loved Bryan. He would do anything for his younger brother. Yet when his younger brother got into his things, stole his money, wrote all over his baseball cards and his wall, their parents had to intervene. They moved Bryan into a small room across the hall that originally had served as a storage room. Nowadays, they might diagnose Bryan's condition as attention deficit disorder, but years ago there weren't a lot of resources for hyperactive kids.

On this night, Alec tried to put those thoughts out of his mind. He sat on the edge of the bed and opened up the yearbook to the back page. He stared down at the message written there. *Megan will always be mine.* This didn't look like Bryan's handwriting—and Alec should know. Alec had seen many of Bryan's letters and school papers. Alec had helped his younger brother with his homework. He would get the handwriting analyzed. He made a note of it, and added it to the e-mail to Steve.

He turned to the front of the book and stared down at a picture of Megan. It was true what he had said to her tonight, he was happy she was with him. But deep in his soul he felt it was more than that. Could he be falling back in love with her all over again? He had told her things he had not told anyone, why he went to police work, his concern for his mother. And she had listened so intently, her gaze almost comforting. She knew what it was to hurt.

But there was that one thing that was stopping him.

The lie.

Maybe it's time to tell her everything. No. He couldn't. He couldn't lose her again. He just couldn't risk it.

He had lied for his brother. He had committed perjury in court on the witness stand and nobody knew. Nobody except his brother. Was that why he always felt so protective of him? Was that why he helped him even now? Sent him money when he needed it? Was that why he was worried that Bryan was the only one who could expose him? Was he worried about what Bryan held over his head?

After Megan's grandmother accused Bryan of pushing her, Bryan had come to Alec. "You remember that night, bro. You remember when I came home that night. I wasn't out at her grandmother's house. The people are going to say I was. People are going to say all sorts of things. But I can't tell them where I really was. You gotta trust me. You got to tell them I was with you. Because I was. You know I was." His voice was staccato and breathless and he literally jumped from foot to foot as if he was on drugs. Alec asked him if he was.

"No. No. No, I'm not. Because I didn't do it, ya know. I didn't. You gotta help me. You gotta."

Alec knew that he would. He would protect his brother like he had protected him all these years.

Later, in court, he would say he had spent the evening shooting pool with his brother. But the timeline was off and he knew it. Back then, Alec didn't believe his brother had pushed Megan's grandmother to her death. His brother wouldn't tell him where he had really been that night, only that he didn't do it. Alec believed him, then. So did their mother. Their father hadn't said much. He never did where Bryan was concerned. He mostly just holed himself up at work and pretended that problems with Bryan didn't exist.

What did Alec think now? He honestly didn't know. Maybe no one would ever know the truth. His brother had gone to jail. Justice had been served. In the end, his perjury hadn't mattered. But he had betrayed Megan. And when she had walked away, pregnant with their baby, he knew he didn't deserve to go after her.

How could he tell her the truth now? If he wanted Megan in his life, then he knew he would have to continue to keep his secret. He looked out at the moon and made a decision. God had forgiven him his sin. Justice had been done. The whole thing was long over. Megan didn't need to know. She need never know. But why did that resolution make him feel so miserable?

He went back to the desk and retrieved a manila envelope from the bottom drawer. It was the kind of envelope with a string and toggle. He unwound the string and pulled out a picture, a five-by-seven color photo of himself and Megan. It had been taken at the winter dance, a few months before they were to be married. She had pulled the sides of her long hair up into a glittery barrette on the top of her head, and the ends of her hair softly curled around her shoulders. Her dress was light blue, caught in at the waist by a wide ribbon. It fell to the floor in satiny folds. She looked happy and confident. She was also pregnant in the picture, but neither of them knew that when this picture was taken.

He stood next to her, awkward and skinny and miles taller than she was. He wore a flower on his lapel of the same flower variety as the corsage she wore on her wrist. Whenever he stayed in this room, he looked at this picture.

If he remembered correctly, it was Bryan who had taken the picture. Bryan had been happy for the two of them. Smiling, he had slapped Alec on the back. Alec had winced away from this slap, which seemed more like a punch. "Hey Bryan, easy there, brother."

Bryan had laughed and said, "The best man won. I'm just happy for you, bro. Meggie is a great kid."

"She is."

"Besides, you already know she was never my girlfriend. We've only ever been good friends, and I've already moved on."

And he had. By that time he was dating a girl named Olive. That didn't last long. He now had a Christian girlfriend and they planned to marry.

A girl that Megan said she recognized.

There was a gentle knock on his door. Alec put the picture away before he rose to open the door. His mother stood there, pale and agitated. She said, "I just wanted to make sure you have everything you need."

"I'm fine, Mother. Thank you."

She remained standing there. It was obvious to Alec that there was something more on her mind.

"What is it, Mother?"

"I'm worried about your brother. When I talk to him, I feel I'm talking to a brick. I ask him about work, about Lorena, and he never answers my questions directly. I want to know when they're getting married and I never get an answer."

"I spoke with him, Mother. He's fine." Alec could understand his brother's attitude. His mother could be clingy and whiny at times. No wonder Bryan was backing away.

"But with these murders, I can't help but worry. About both my boys."

"Both of us are fine."

She swallowed a few times before she said, "There's something wrong with his girlfriend."

"Lorena?"

"Have you ever met her? On one of your trips to see your brother?"

Alec shook his head. Lorena was relatively new.

His mother bit her lip. "There's just something funny about that woman. I don't altogether trust her, if you must know. On the phone, Bryan goes on and on about her, how they're going to get married. But I've never so much as talked to her on the phone. If he phones and happens to say that Lorena is there making supper or something and I ask to speak to her, she's always too busy to come to the phone. I don't trust her. I fear that Bryan is been taking taken advantage of. I have a favor to ask, Alec…"

He waited. He knew what was coming.

"Can you…?" She paused. "I mean, you're a policeman. Can you maybe look her up? You know…" She waved one hand. "On those files that you have?" She placed a piece of paper on the desk next to him. "This is all the information I have on her."

Alec looked at it. It contained her name—Lorena Street—and an e-mail address. "The thing that has me wondering is that I sent her an e-mail. Now I get so confused with e-mail and stuff, so I know I could have done it wrong, but it didn't seem to get to her. Just as soon as I sent it the e-mail came back to my own in-box. Does that make sense?"

"Maybe this is an old e-mail address. You don't have a street address?"

She shook her head. "This is all that I have. I asked Bryan once where she lived, but he never answered me. That's what I mean about him."

Alec sighed. How many times had Alec done this? Pulled strings when it came to his own brother? First there was the lie, but it didn't end there. It never did. He had loaned his brother money. Had Bryan ever paid him back? Maybe once or twice in ten years. And then there was his work. More than once, Alec had intervened for his brother by phoning Bryan's employer in New Mexico, or he'd flown down there and talked with his landlord, and then reminded Bryan that he had to write out a check on the first of every month.

Yet when Alec went to church with Bryan, people seemed to know him, to accept him, and he was never without a lot of Sunday lunch invitations. "I'm trying, bro," Bryan would say. "With Jesus's help I'm going to make it."

When Alec would urge him to move closer to home, Bryan would vehemently shake his head. "Can't, bro. Too many people know me there. I'm making a new start here."

"Okay, Mother," he told her now. "I'll take care of it."

After she left, he sat at the little boy's school desk in the corner of his old bedroom and put his head in his hands. Sure, he wanted Megan back in his life, but would his brother, his family, always have to come first?

The next day Alec and Megan arrived at the home of Madeline Magill, Paul's wife. It was the day before Paul's funeral. Megan had never met Madeleine since the woman was someone Paul had met at college.

They were met at the door by a small, round woman who introduced herself as being from Paul and Madeline's church.

She opened the door for them. "Are you Alec?" she asked.

When Alec said he was, she said, "Madeline is in the kitchen. The children are down in the family room with some of the kids from church."

Alec guided Megan through the house. "The kitchen's back here," he said.

"You've been here before."

"A few times. Paul and Madeline invited me to their home a couple of times. We tried to keep up the friendship, but they have kids and were involved in different things than me. After a while we had nothing in common. And then I moved to Whisper Lake Crossing."

They went into the kitchen where a woman about Megan's age was sitting at the table, back straight, hands in her lap, staring straight ahead. Several people bustled about and behind her, washing up dishes, clearing up food, setting more food out. Her eyes appeared red-rimmed, but she smiled when she saw it was Alec who had entered the room.

"Alec," she said. "I'm so glad you came. All the way from Whisper Lake. It's been so long. I don't think I've ever been up there. I've heard it's nice. Paul and I always meant to go…"

"Madeline." He went to her. She rose and he hugged her lightly and gave her a peck on one cheek. "I am so sorry," he said. Then her grasp on him became tighter. He held her firmly while her shoulders heaved.

When Megan was introduced and conveyed her condolences, Madeline said,

"You mean *the* Megan? Paul told me about everything that happened with your wedding. I'm glad that you and Alec ended up together in the end. At least one of us is lucky." Her eyes filled with tears and Megan didn't have the heart to correct her. Neither did Alec.

"Why don't you sit down? As you can see, I've got plenty of food. It just keeps coming. The church is keeping me well supplied. And someone's always making fresh coffee. Help yourself," Madeline said.

Alec did so, and poured three cups of coffee.

Megan said, "I knew Paul from a long time ago. He was a good friend of ours."

"His death came so soon after Jennifer's," Madeline interjected. "It's funny how you can live in the same town even, and lose track of people...." She looked up at Alec. "Remember those times together? You and Paul and Jennifer and her husband Sam and me? You called them reunion parties..."

"Another girl who was to be in the wedding party also died," Alec said. "Do you remember Paul talking about a girl named Sophia?"

Madeline nodded.

When Alec told her that Sophia had died the same way as Paul and Jennifer she expressed shock, and raised one eyebrow in her expressive face. The woman washing dishes behind her suddenly stopped, as if she were listening.

Madeline said, "Maybe that's why that police officer was questioning me so thoroughly. He asked if Paul had any enemies. Had anything strange been happening that day or two before he died? Had I seen anyone lurking about? Paul had just taken the car in to have the oil changed. So I would've assumed the mechanic would check the brakes, wouldn't you? That's what I told the police. I assume they went and talked with the mechanic, but I haven't heard anything. But that's what it was, wasn't it, brakes that failed? How can that be?"

"I'm here as your friend," Alec said, "but I'm also here to try to find out what happened to Paul, because we think the same thing happened to Sophia and Jennifer."

"You think…" Madeline said. "You think Paul may have been…killed? Intentionally?"

Alec leaned toward her, his elbows on the table. "This is very important, Madeline. Have you seen anyone around? Anyone lurking at all? Any stranger at the door? Even one person?"

She shook her head. "The police asked me that. I said no. I can't remember anything unusual. I never saw anything—"

"I did." All three faces looked up to the doorway. Standing there was a big woman in a denim jumper with salt-and-pepper hair pulled tightly back from her face. She stood uncertainly in the doorway.

"You did?" Alec asked

"Yes. I live across the street." She entered the kitchen. "My name is Polly. The police never asked me any questions. I thought Paul's death was an accident. But I remember seeing someone."

"Please," he said. "Sit down, Polly."

Nervously she sat down across from Madeleine. Polly reached out and touched Madeline's wrist. "I'm so sorry, Maddie." Then to Alec, she said, "We've been neighbors for twelve years. Our kids played together. If I had any idea…"

"Please," he said writing in his note-book. "You said you saw someone? Or something?"

"I saw someone. It could have been nothing, I don't know. But I heard you talking and I remembered. A couple of weeks ago, it was the middle of the night and I couldn't sleep so I got up and made tea."

"What did you see?" Madeline asked. "Did you see someone in our garage?"

She looked from Madeline to Alec. "I took my tea to the living room window…."

Alec put his hand up. "Can you tell me what day this was?"

She told him. He wrote it down.

"Do you know what time it was?" he asked.

"It was three thirty-three. I remember it exactly. I looked at the time on the DVD player and thought that it was funny that I was up and sitting in my living room chair at exactly three thirty-three."

Alec urged her to continue.

"I took my tea to the window and looked at the streetlight." She paused.

"And you saw someone? Someone saw you?" This came from Madeline.

Polly shook her head. "No. Nothing like that. I saw a movement under the streetlight. It frightened me because you don't often see people walking around in the middle of the night in this neighborhood. I saw a man and he was walking slowly. He kept going down the street until he disappeared."

"Did you get a look at him?" Alec asked.

"I watched him," she said. "My lights were off. He couldn't see me, so I watched him. I would say he was medium build." She looked at Alec. "About your size. Thin. Tall. He wore a long dark coat. No hat. And, I rcmember his hair."

"Hair?" Madeline asked. "What about his hair?"

"It was thick and very dark. I would say black. Either that or dark, dark brown."

Megan glanced up at Alec sharply. The man who had delivered the invitation to her at the Schooner Café had black hair, so dark and so thick that Marlene had mentioned it specifically.

Alec was writing rapidly.

"Polly," Alec said, looking up at her. "Do you think we could go over to your house and you could show me exactly where you saw this person?"

Polly nodded.

"I'll come," Megan said.

"I'll come, too," Madeline said.

The four of them tromped through the snow across the street to where Polly lived. When they got to her living room, the precise window she'd been sitting at, Alec took command and asked questions that put her at ease, yet got the information he needed. Megan's admiration for this man was growing.

Polly pointed out exactly where the man had walked to and from. No, she hadn't seen a car, she said. The man walked slowly and seemed to pause at each driveway, ever so slightly before moving on to the next one.

She said, "I thought at first he had a dog from the way he kept stopping and starting. But he didn't. Oh, Maddie, I should have remembered this. I had no idea Paul's car had been tampered with. If I'd had any idea...oh, this is simply terrible."

Alec took down more of Polly's information and told her that someone from the local police department would be contacting her. He gave her his card, told her to contact him if she remembered anything more, and they made their way back to Madeline's house. Alec hugged Madeline once more and then they left.

"Black hair," Megan said as Alec drove away from the neighborhood. "The guy who dropped the invitation to me had black hair."

"I know."

The school yearbook and guest list were on the backseat and Megan brought them to her lap. "Who do we know from the old days who had black hair?" She thumbed through the book, paying special attention to the three people who had police records.

Of the three people, Jeff's hair was fair and Daniel's head was shaved. Only Anna had black hair.

But both Marlene and Polly had seen a man. They were probably back at square one.

NINE

The sighting of the black-haired man was new information, and Detective Brantley Peterson of the Augusta Police Department listened with interest as Alec told him again about the invitations, the wedding that never happened, and why. Alec laid it all out, finally. Some of the story had been held back in his previous conversation with the detective who handled Jennifer's accident, but it was time that the police knew about his connection to what was going on.

It was just the three of them in Peterson's office. Megan didn't say anything. They were sitting side by side in chairs, so Alec couldn't see the particular expression on her face, and he could only guess what she was thinking. He didn't look at her as he told Peterson about the death of Megan's grandmother.

Detective Peterson took down the particulars and wanted to know more about Megan's grandmother's death. He was going to look up the files and reports about that case, he said.

Megan asked, "Do you think these deaths are somehow connected to my grandmother?"

"We don't know," he said. "There might or might not be a connection. We won't know until we go down that road for a while." To Alec he said, "And your brother, he has maintained his innocence to this day?"

Alec said he had.

"So maybe we're looking at something else," Detective Peterson suggested.

Megan said, "I think so, because if the person who killed my grandmother got away with it—presuming they did—why stir all this up now? Twenty years after the fact?"

Detective Peterson shrugged and Alec shook his head.

"We're dealing with a serial killer," Detective Peterson said.

Alec jerked his head in the detective's direction.

"Three deaths. Same MO. It might be time to call in the FBI."

Alec swallowed slowly. If the FBI became involved, his perjury would certainly be made known. There would be no way around that. As well, the FBI surely would question Bryan. He didn't know if he was ready to come forward with everything just yet.

Detective Peterson wrote down Bryan's telephone number and address. He also made a copy of the wedding guest list and all the information Megan and Alec had gathered so far. He promised Alec he would keep in touch. He shook their hands and they said goodbye.

On the way to Bath, Maine, Megan said, "It might be Saul Kluffas."

Lost in his own thoughts, Alec was momentarily baffled by her comment. "Who is Saul Kluffas?"

"He has black hair. I sort of remember him."

"I don't."

"He worked on the high school yearbook

with me. I think he liked me. A friend told me he had a crush on me."

"Everyone had a crush on you at one time or another." If everyone who ever liked Megan was a suspect, their list would be long indeed.

The back of her neck reddened. "You give me too much credit. I think most people just felt sorry for me because my parents died and I was an only child who grew up with my grandmother."

Just before the turnoff to Bath, Alec surprised himself by saying, "Do you think…do you think there might be a chance for us? For the two of us? Now? I'd love it if we could explore that a bit. Just to see where it leads."

Why had he just asked her that? Was it because last night, when he had said goodnight, he had briefly touched her hand? Was it because, despite what had come between him, he could sense that she felt the same way about him?

She shook her head and looked away. "I don't know. Maybe too much time has passed. The one thing I've learned is that a person can never go back and change the past."

He sighed. What about going forward? He wanted to know. But maybe she was right. You can never go back, yet these murders were forcing them to do just that.

"I'm just not the girl you remember," she said.

"But you are," he said, after some thought. "You are the girl I fell in love with." Later, he said, "I wish I could go back and undo things."

"Like I said, you can never go back." After a moment she asked, "Do you still go to church? Do you mind me asking?"

"I don't mind at all. My relationship with God is important to me. It's a journey. I've not yet arrived."

She said, "I've not arrived, either. I'm not even out the gate. Sometimes I have this idea that God is still punishing me, that he punished me by taking my parents and then my grandmother and next my baby. That's an idea I can't get out of my head. The girl you remember then had her life all figured out and planned ahead of her. The woman I am now doesn't know a thing."

"You still have that soft center, Megan, that concern for people. You were so good with my mother all through the dinner yesterday."

"I felt sorry for her. She seemed so lost. So thin and jittery. I guess we all carry things that at times feel too heavy for us."

"I guess we do."

He looked at her sadly. She was so out of reach. He wanted to offer her comfort, give her some great words of wisdom, but how could he when he couldn't share with her the one thing that was uppermost on his mind. They were getting near the residential streets of her old house in Bath, Maine. "You'll have to direct me here," he said, looking at the road signs. "What was the address?"

She told him.

Together they navigated toward town using the map he'd downloaded from the Internet.

"My mother's been like that for a while, anxious. I told you that she worries about Bryan. She's also worried about my dad. She carries a lot, or feels she has to carry a lot."

"I guess that would be difficult," Megan

said. "Losing a child." Her voice was a whisper. "Losing a child is always difficult. No matter what the circumstances."

He reached over and laid a hand on top of her clenched fists. He expected her to stiffen, but she didn't. She seemed to soften. He kept his hand there. He could sense her trembling as they began to drive down the road to the house Megan had lived in for the first five years of her life. He stopped when he came to it, but kept the car engine running for warmth.

From her purse she extracted the picture that had been e-mailed to her. This was the same place. They both could see it. Except for the snow it was exactly like the picture. He turned off the engine.

"What should we do?" She looked at him expectantly.

"We'll go and talk to the people who live there now. Maybe they know who took the picture."

"What if the black-haired man lives there?" She shuddered.

"Then we'll find out, won't we?" But he wasn't as confident as he made himself sound. What if the black-haired man did live there? Should he have called for some kind of backup?

"Okay, then. Let's go." She opened her door and hopped out.

Picture in hand, they walked up the plowed driveway. Alec pressed the doorbell. People had been here. Lots of people. There was an abundance of footprints and tire prints. No one seemed to be here now, though. No one came to the door.

There was no movement from inside the house. He rang the doorbell again, but there was no answer. As they were making their way back to the car, a woman from next door came racing out toward them, waving her arms and calling. She wore a long purple housecoat, pink sponge curlers and, despite the snow encrusted banks, her thick calloused feet were stuffed into a pair of floppy mules.

"Yoo-hoo!" she called and waved. "Are you here about the house? They put me in charge of it. They're in Florida for the winter."

Alec unfolded the picture. "Actually, we're looking for the person who took this picture. Have you seen someone around taking pictures of the house?"

"He might've had black hair," Megan added. Alec silenced her with a look. The one thing you didn't do in police work was put ideas in people's heads.

"Black hair?"

The woman pulled her glasses up onto her nose and peered down at the picture.

"That picture? I don't know anything about black hair, but maybe Claudia took it. Or Maxine. Could've been Bill. I've met all of them in the past week. Wait a minute," she said raising her forefinger. "I think it was Marcus who took this one. You should see Marcus. Very handsome guy."

All of this was making Alec's head spin. "Who exactly are those people?" Alec asked.

The woman looked at him with surprise in her eyes. "The real estate people. I've met them all in the past week. But, if I can be honest, I think they're asking way too much for the house in today's economy." She shook her head from side to side. "Too much. But don't tell anyone I said that. I'm only saying that because you two seem like a nice young couple. The neighborhood could sure use some nice young people like you two."

Megan said, "This is a real estate picture?"

"Right. It's on the Internet too, and it's been in the paper. Especially when they had that open house last Saturday. Tons of people came to look at it."

"The house is for sale," Alec said thoughtfully. "How come there's no sign?" he asked.

The woman waved her hand. "That's the Randolsons for you. They don't want people knowing they're away and their house is for sale. Don't ask me why."

"How long have you lived here?" Alec asked.

"Coming on fifteen years. I bought the place right after my husband Roger died. I've been living here ever since. If you want the place, you'd better hurry. I heard there's an offer on it."

"An offer?" Alec raised his eyebrows.

"That's what the neighbors are saying."

"Can you tell me, Mrs....?"

"Woolenstook. Marva Woolenstook." She extended her hand.

"I'm Alec Black, Mrs. Woolenstook, and

this is Megan Brooks. You wouldn't happen to know who made this offer, would you?"

She shook her head so vigorously that one of her pink curlers fell out onto the snowbank. She bent way over to pick it up. When she had risen to full height, she said, "Couldn't tell you. I'm not even sure if what I have is accurate information. I heard it from Flo Fisher across the street, but that woman is a gossip, so I don't know if it's true or not."

"Can you tell us which real estate firm the house is listed with?"

She told him and gave him directions to get there.

They thanked her and left.

Later in the car Megan said, "How much you want to bet that the black-haired man is the one who made the offer."

"Well," said Alec as they made their way downtown, "we're about to find out."

When Alec and Megan arrived at the real estate office and expressed interest in the property, the woman named Maxine ushered them into her office while extolling the virtues of the property.

"We understood," Alec said, "that there's been an offer made on that place."

She looked up at them. "Where did you hear that?"

Megan said, "From a neighbor."

"Marva?" The woman made a dismissive gesture with her hand. "You can't believe a word she says. That woman likes to gossip. No, there is no offer currently pending on that property. I could show the house to you today, if you like. The owners are away."

"Was there an offer on it at one time?" he asked.

"We had someone interested in the property but they ended up not coming up with the financing."

He regarded her. "They? Or him?"

Maxine leaned back in her chair and said, "Excuse me?"

"Who was it?" Megan asked.

She shook her head. "I'm really not at liberty to say."

It was time to stop the charade. "We're not looking for a house," Alec said. "I'm a police officer." He got out his badge and ID and showed them to her. "We're looking for someone." He described the man that both Marlene and Polly had seen and asked Maxine if anyone with this description had been through the house.

She looked from one to the other. "Well, I don't know, Officer. Lots of people have been shown the house." Was it his imagination or was she becoming cagey and cautious?

"Black hair," Megan said. "He would have had noticeable thick, black hair."

"As I said, there have been a lot of people who've gone through that house. I would imagine that quite a few of them had thick, black hair."

"This would be a single man, someone alone," Alec added.

"This is really important," Megan said. "Have you had some open houses? Sometimes there are guest books at those."

Alec wondered if this conversation was hopeless. If the black-haired man had been clever enough to kill three people, then he would not be so stupid as to sign a guest book with his real name.

"We've had lots of open houses. And yes, I have guest books," Maxine said.

"Would you mind showing them to us?" Alec asked.

After a short pause, where she appeared to be weighing his question, she said, "Yes, I would mind. Do you have a warrant for this sort of thing?"

When Alec realized there was no more to be gained here without a warrant, he cut the conversation short, thanked Maxine and said goodbye. "And if you change your mind about the guest book, please give me a call." He laid a business card on her desk and he and Megan left.

"So," Megan said later in the car. "Whoever sent me the picture just copied it off the Internet? I really don't think he made an offer at all."

"You could be right. Then again, he could be the person who couldn't get financing."

The sky was still light when they pulled into a fast-food restaurant in Bangor. They both ordered cheeseburgers. He remembered she loved cheeseburgers. Over their quick meal they reviewed the case, the yearbook, the guest list and what they thought they had accomplished. Maybe not a lot. Maybe more than they knew.

He wanted to ask her again if she thought there was a chance for them. But he didn't. He couldn't. Right now it was enough to be with her.

"In answer to your question about whether there's a chance for us—maybe," Megan said as they walked back to the car together.

He felt his heart soar.

Later as they neared the exit that led to a large rest area and campground, Alec drove that way on a whim.

"Where we going?" she asked.

"Time to stretch my legs. Long legs and a short car make for a long trip," he said.

He took the road that led down to the campsite and rest area. Everything was closed, of course, but he knew that from this place they could see Mount Katahdin. He pointed it out to Megan.

"Do you remember Mount Katahdin, Meggie?"

"How could I forget?"

They couldn't drive too far. The road had

only been minimally plowed. When they got as far as the plowing would allow, Alec stopped the car. They got out and walked a few hundred feet. From this vantage point they had a clear view of the snowcapped mountain that had meant so much to them at one time.

Her eyes on Mount Katahdin, Megan said, "Of course I remember that mountain. I could never forget that trail, and hiking with all the kids." She smiled. "I never thought I would make it."

They talked for a while, reminiscing about the group of kids who had hiked up the mountain with them on that day. Alec surprised himself by even mentioning a few specific names. They stood in companionable quiet together remembering the day it all began for them.

"That was a good summer," he said.

"A very good summer." She wasn't looking at him when she said this. Her gaze instead had turned toward the mountain. He touched her hair and gently turned her face toward him. He looked down into her blue eyes.

"Your eyes. Such a pretty color. I don't

remember them being that way. Maybe it's because you wore glasses then."

She leaned back from him and laughed. "They're contact lenses, Alec. You can get them in all different colors. If you get close enough, you can tell they're contacts."

He put one hand on her hair and drew her to him. Their lips found each other as if by instinct.

The kiss seemed to take both of them by surprise.

On the way back to the car, he took her hand and said, "I know this is awkward."

"But lovely just the same," she said.

They held hands as they made their way back to his car in the cold. He wished it could stay like this, just him and Megan, the way it used to be.

But it wasn't. It never would be. As he got back in the driver's seat he realized just how far they were from normalcy.

He had just kissed the woman he loved, yet a murderer was still out there, a murderer who could be following them at this very moment. He adjusted his mirror and headed back toward Whisper Lake Crossing.

Why did that dark thought intrude upon his thinking right now? He tried to push it aside, but while he held Megan's hand he remembered the line in the back cover of Bryan's yearbook. *Megan will always be mine.* Why had he been so quick to say it wasn't Bryan's handwriting?

The truth was that he wasn't sure.

The rest of the way home Megan thought about that kiss and about Alec. She thought about the almost tentative way his mouth had probed hers. He had called it "awkward." And it certainly was. It was because she didn't know what it meant or how she really felt. He had wanted to know if there was a chance for them. She wanted there to be, but she was afraid. When they got back into Alec's car, they didn't talk much. It was as if they were both trying to process what had happened back there. They were attracted to each other, that much was for certain, but could she trust him? Could she trust her rapidly beating heart? Could she trust anyone? She didn't know the answer to that.

She needed to come to terms with the

past. But on cold, lonely nights, her mind would go back to the day that her grandmother fell. Alec and his mother and father had come to the hospital when she had frantically called them. They sat with her and talked with the police about the suspicious fall. But then her grandmother, in her feeble voice, had pointed to Alec's parents and said, "Your son did this. He pushed me." Megan had immediately gasped, looking at Alec, her hand on her mouth.

Instead of saying something like, "That's not true," Alec had gotten red in the face, stood up and walked out of the hospital room with not a word to anyone. After a moment of surprise, his parents had followed him.

Her grandmother quickly corrected herself and said, "Not Alec. The other one. Bryan." But by this time Megan was alone in the room.

At the time, it seemed that Alec knew something about her grandmother's fall, something he wasn't telling her.

She looked over at him. Because she had to know she asked, "You never told me in so many words, but do you still think your brother is innocent?"

It took him a long time to answer, so long that she actually looked away from him and at the white scenery speeding by. His silence said it all. He still didn't believe his brother had pushed her.

His answer then surprised her. "I don't know." He said each word carefully, clearly. He shook his head slowly and said it again. "I really don't know. At the time, yes, I thought he was innocent, because I couldn't imagine why he would do anything to harm your grandmother. She was a lovely lady. It made no sense. But in the years that have passed, I have wondercd." She nodded up at him and swallowed. "I'm being honest with you, Megan."

"Does your mother think Bryan is innocent?"

"She says she does, but there are times when I think she's saying that just because she feels she is supposed to and not because she really believes it anymore." He said, "She has one son who is a convicted killer and one son who is a cop."

Megan measured her words carefully. "And you feel you have to always be the one to give him the benefit of the doubt?"

Alec looked at her, his dark eyes hooded. "Someone has to."

Megan closed her eyes. Nothing had changed. This was something they wouldn't get past. He had apologized for not being there for her, for leaving her and the baby, but his family would always come first. She realized this now.

It hurt her so profoundly that this man who had just kissed her so tenderly still didn't quite believe her. She knew that if Alec had to do it over again, he would probably make exactly the same decision that he had twenty years ago.

This would always be between them.

She turned away from him, blinking away hot tears. She was remembering. There was always a darkness stirring just beneath the surface of Bryan's eyes. They would be joking and laughing, having a wonderful time and Megan might say something that she thought was pretty funny and suddenly Bryan would get a serious look on his face and say, "Megan, that's not funny." And he was serious. In short, she was a little afraid of him. That's why they only went out a few times. She never told this to Alec.

Even when Bryan came along on their dates, she didn't complain that sometimes she was afraid of him.

You don't mind do you that he comes along on our picnic? He's had a bit of a rough day.

Sure, sure, I don't mind.

She could tell Alec wanted to kiss her when he dropped her at her cabin at Trail's End. And she felt so drawn to him that she wanted him to. And then she forced herself to get back in control. She backed away from him, fled inside her cabin and closed the door behind her. From around the edge of the curtain she could see the way he looked at the cabin door, puzzled for a few minutes, before he drove away.

Earlier she had toyed with the idea of inviting him in for a cup of coffee by the fireplace, but not now. She decided to e-mail her godmother Eunice. She needed to talk to a friend. Even if it was only by e-mail. Plus, someone should know that she was really here and not holed up in her apartment in Baltimore.

She ended up telling her godmother all about Alec, the murders, everything.

Her phone rang at ten-thirty and eagerly she answered it thinking the only person it could be was Eunice. They would have a good, long talk. Maybe Eunice would even pray for her over the phone like she did sometimes.

"Hello," she answered.

"Hey there," said a male voice she didn't recognize.

"Hello?"

"This is Brad from next door. Welcome home." He chuckled and in her mind she could see the glimmer of those big, white teeth.

"Thanks."

"Hey, have you had a chance to cook up a Web design for me yet?"

"Not yet. I've been away all day. Just got home."

"Not just all day, but all night, too. We

came over. You weren't there. Place was all locked up. We were worried about you."

Megan was momentarily irked. She was a grown woman after all. She said, "I'm fine. Why would you be worried about me?"

"Oh." He chuckled again. It was a big and hearty sound. "Not me so much, but Vicky. You know Vicky. She can be a mother hen at times."

No, I don't know Vicky. What Megan didn't need right now, with threats and murders on her mind, was someone she didn't even know worrying about her.

"Vicky really was worried. Especially when your car was there all night and you weren't. We thought maybe you'd gone out hiking and got lost in the woods. I thought of checking with Steve and Nori. Vicky was ready to call the police," Brad said.

Megan softened. Maybe this was just honest concern. She wasn't used to people, other than Eunice, worrying about her. Maybe that's all this was. "I'm sorry that you were worried. I'm fine, really," she said.

"So," he said. "What about my Web site?"

"Brad, look, some things have been

happening. If I'm still here a week from now, then maybe we could get together and go over it. Maybe after my own business here is done."

"What business do you have here in the middle of winter, sugar?"

"Personal business. Uh, Brad, I'm not really comfortable with people calling me *sugar*."

He laughed. "Oh. Sorry. That's just me. I call everybody *sugar*. That's what my mother called me. But I'll try to remember not to call you *sugar* ever again."

"I would appreciate it."

"Hey," he said. "What about right now? I'm still up. So, apparently, are you. If I came over there, I could show you what I want in terms of a Web site."

At ten-thirty at night? Megan tried to keep her voice light. In her line of work, she never wanted to turn away business. She needed every penny. But she also didn't want a strange man coming over to her place at ten-thirty at night. "I'd love to Brad, but right now I'm afraid you wouldn't get your money's worth. I'm so exhausted I'm not thinking straight."

"I understand. Sorry if I intruded. I'm really sorry about that. Sometimes I need someone to give me a good punch to the back of my neck. I live on my own. That's why I need a good woman to keep me in line." More chuckles.

A good woman? She was beginning to doubt whether she needed this guy's business bad enough. "That's okay," she said.

"You have a nice night and pleasant dreams."

"Same to you," she said.

"And if you dream about me I won't mind."

She blinked and said goodbye. No, he definitely was not the kind of guy she wanted invading her space at ten-thirty at night. Before she went back to her e-mail, she made sure her curtains were drawn tightly and that her door was locked, and the dead bolts secured.

She sat on her bed, her computer in her lap, and clicked through some links. One client's Web site was nearly completed. All she had to do was come up with a few more bits of artwork for one of the links. She would concentrate on that now, instead of thinking about Brad.

Twenty minutes later she knew exactly why Bryan's girlfriend Lorena had looked so familiar. She gazed down at the picture on her screen for several minutes. It was close to midnight. She wondered if she should phone Alec this late. Even though this probably had nothing to do with the murders, Alec should know. His mother should know.

There, on the computer screen, was Lorena. That same bored, pouty expression. That same stance. Except that in this picture, she wasn't leaning up against a palm tree, she was leaning against a fence. Same picture. Just manipulated from that setting to this one.

Lorena, Bryan's girlfriend, was not a real person. Megan regularly used stock photography for her work. In her surfing this evening, she had found "Lorena" at a site that assembled faces from stock photos to be purchased for use in products and advertisements. The name of this particular made-up woman was "Mandy."

Megan was puzzled. Alec's mother said that Bryan had met Lorena online. She seemed to indicate that the two were getting married, that they knew each other well. But that was impossible. She tapped her fingers on her computer. It was one of two things, she thought. Either the so-called Lorena was leading him on, or else Bryan was lying.

She bookmarked the page and then went to bed. She made a mental note to call Alec first thing in the morning. Even though their future was looking more and more doubtful, he should know this.

Hours later, a knock at the door woke her.

Sleepy-eyed, she forced herself up. The knock was insistent. Through the window, she saw the early-morning gray. She threw on her robe, tied it around her, ran a hand through her hair and went to the door.

A deliveryman stood on her front step with armloads and armloads of flowers. So full and so huge were the blossoms, she could barely see his face behind them. But what she did see of him was grinning widely.

"A delivery," he managed to say over the top of the riot of colors.

"What? Here? At my *cabin?*" *Were these from Alec? Could it be?*

She smoothed her hair out of her face. She couldn't believe her eyes.

"Is this the cabin named Grace?"

"Yes," she said.

"I was instructed to get these to the Trail's End cabin called Grace by seven this morning. No later. The guy paid extra."

Alec, she thought. He had discerned how upset she was yesterday. The flowers meant that he finally believed her. She touched her mouth and remembered the kiss.

The delivery guy continued, "Whoever sent them must think you're pretty special. Do you have a vase? Or two? You're going to need more than one."

"I have no idea what this cabin has." She took one of the bouquets from his arms and laid them on the counter.

She took the other bouquet and placed it beside the first one.

"Sign here," he said.

She did so. "Who are they from?" she asked innocently, although of course she knew.

"There's a note in that first batch of flowers over there."

She saw it, the tiny square envelope had her name on it—Meggie. She smiled to herself. His name for her.

After the delivery guy left, she found four quart-size large-mouthed canning jars. She filled each with water and divided up the flowers. There were roses, violets, mums, baby's breath.

She placed two jars on the kitchen table and the other two on the coffee table. Then, standing next to the counter, she opened the little flowered note card and read it.

The moan that came from her mouth seemed to emanate from someplace deep within her very core. Fingers quivering, she dropped the card as if it burned. She reached to the table to steady herself as she fell, whimpering, quivering to the floor. As she did so, she knocked over one of the mason jars of flowers. It broke at her feet, glass shards, water and petals scattering everywhere beside her. And the note staring up at her in block letters: ABORTION IS A SIN!!

TEN

An hour later, there was another knock on her door. Megan ignored it. Her suitcase was open on her bed and she was flinging clothes into it. She had managed to clean up the broken glass, the spilled water and the leaves. She emptied the mason jars, rinsed them out and put them away. She swept the huge bundle of flowers and the offending note into the sports section of the newspaper, wrapped everything up and put it all into the trash can beside her back door. Then she had mopped up the floor.

As she worked, she came to a decision. She might be drawn to Alec in ways she didn't want to think about, but it wasn't worth it. First of all, she was in danger. The note proved it. And second, she didn't trust herself around Alec. He would only hurt her again and she didn't want to stick around for that. She would pack up today and get out of here before the storm came. Her tormentor knew exactly where she was now. He knew exactly who she was. She needed to get going. Hadn't there been enough warnings? The shooting on the lake? The invitation dropped off for her? Now this. She'd had none of this in Baltimore. She needed to get home.

The persistent knock on her door had interrupted her thoughts. It was probably Brad, she thought, come to look at Web designs. When the knocking didn't stop, she decided to answer the door. She would go and firmly tell Brad that she couldn't do his Web site because she was leaving.

However, it was not Brad. It was Alec at the door and he was wearing some sort of a strange one-piece spacesuit getup that looked like it belonged on the moon. Her face must have betrayed something. "Megan, what's wrong?" he asked as he entered the cabin.

"What are you wearing?" she asked.

"A snowmobile suit," he said. "A snow-mobile is the best way to get where I'm going. My deputy Stu loaned it to me. I got a call that someone saw a truck abandoned way out near Twin Peaks Island. The fishing shacks are across from that. My thought is that this could maybe be the truck I saw the first day we met."

"The guy who was shooting at us, you mean."

"Right." He seemed to notice her suit-cases for the first time and her already packed up computer. "You're leaving?" His look seemed to convey surprise, and maybe something underneath that—pain.

"I have to. I have to go now." She was twisting her hands nervously in front of her.

"Is there something wrong? Is your god-mother okay?"

She said, "She's fine. I got flowers. And a note. This morning. I thought maybe…I thought. I could go somewhere else. Change my name. Disappear." She was breathing heavily and could only get out a couple of words at a time. Why was she telling him all this when she had vowed she was leaving? She had wanted to be gone by the time Alec made contact with her again.

"Flowers? What do you mean?"

She took a breath. "A delivery guy brought a huge, and I do mean huge, bouquet of flowers for me this morning."

"Who sent you the flowers? Why did you throw them out?"

"The note that came with them…" She felt as if she would choke. She swallowed several times before she could continue. "It was—horrible. Awful."

"Can I see it?"

She pointed to the back door. "In the garbage can. Just next to the back door."

He went out and came back with her newspaper-wrapped bundle. "Where's this note you're talking about?"

She shrugged. "Somewhere in there. I had to get rid of it. If I'd had a campfire I would've burned everything."

"I'm glad you didn't."

She said, "Be careful of the thorns. There are lots of them."

"There are always lots of thorns."

She sat down on a kitchen chair, suddenly

so weary. She brought her legs up to her on the seat and hugged her knees to her chest. If she didn't maintain some sort of cool, she would turn into a drippy mess of weepy tears. She needed him to leave, but she hoped he would stay. Finally, he unearthed the tiny note card. She watched his eyes as he read it.

After a while he looked up, clearly puzzled. "This came with the flowers?"

"Yep."

"I don't understand what it means, Megan. *Abortion is a sin.* What's all that about?"

She shook her head. "I don't have any idea. It's the next part."

He read the note aloud in its entirety. "'*Abortion is a sin. God forgives sin. We'll have many more children to replace the one you killed.*' What does this mean?"

"I don't understand any of it. But what it means for me is that whoever sent me the flowers knows where I'm staying. He killed my friends. I'm so scared." She was huddled into herself and trembling. He came and pulled up a chair beside her and put his arms around her and held her until her shaking stopped. It felt so safe being there, yet she hated being this conflicted.

A few moments later, he put water in the kettle and set it on her stove to boil. He said, "Can I make something hot for you? Hot chocolate? Coffee? Soup? Something to warm you up?"

"I thought you had an important meeting."

"You're more important, Meggie," he said, reverting to his old name for her. "I've been talking to Steve about this. Could this be someone from your work? Someone who has researched your past? I'm thinking that we should maybe get a copy of your complete client list to Steve. He has channels I don't even have."

"Okay." She nodded. Her client list included a couple of insurance companies, a drama troupe, a bank, a bicycle shop, a couple of rock stars, a sushi bar, none of whom seemed particularly threatening to her. She told Alec this. She thought back to her client correspondence. Nothing seemed out of the ordinary. Everyone paid their bills on time and none of their checks ever bounced. "I don't even know what half my clients look like so one of them could have black hair and I wouldn't know it."

"Steve will know what to do with that list." He added, "I'm just thinking about something else now. Your godmother knew you were pregnant, could she have let it slip? Plus, there would have been doctors and hospital reports. Maybe that's what the note is all about."

"Alec." She almost quivered with anger. "I did not have an abortion. I wanted our baby. How could someone write that? And anyone looking at the hospital records—if they still exist—would know that I carried that baby almost to term. He died in my womb. I didn't know he was sick. I blame myself. I was young and stupid and hurting and I should've gotten better prenatal care."

She was crying again, blubbering and he came and held her once more. He said gently, "You did not kill our child. The baby had a serious heart defect and never had a chance."

"That's what the doctor told me," she said, rubbing her eyes with her fists. "But maybe he was just being kind. Maybe he didn't want to hurt me. And as for Eunice, she wouldn't tell anyone. I know she wouldn't."

The kettle sang. He rose and poured some instant hot chocolate mix into two mugs and then added boiling water.

Megan asked, "How does he know I'm here? I keep a low profile. I've always been really, really careful."

Alec massaged her cold hands between both of his warm ones. "Stu and Steve and I are working night and day on this. Meanwhile," he said, getting up, "I'd like to get this note over to Stu. What was the name of the delivery company that dropped off the flowers?"

She couldn't remember if it was a regular delivery company or a florist van. She shook her head. She just didn't know. The bundle of flowers had blinded her from remembering who it was who had driven them down here. Which is probably what her tormentor had wanted. She said, "The delivery guy didn't have black hair. I do remember that much."

Alec opened up his cell phone and

made a couple of calls. She listened while he told Stu the particulars of the flowers and the note. "Yeah," she heard him say. "I'm heading out on the ice in a few minutes to see what's what." When he closed his cell phone, it rang once. "Messages," he said.

"It's okay," Megan said. "You can answer them. Go ahead. I'll be okay."

He pressed a bunch more buttons on his cell phone and sighed. "Ah, my mother. She's called twice. I haven't been able to connect with her since we got back. She always wants to make sure I'm home safe. I also have a message from Denise. Maybe something to do with the office. I have to head back there later today. Ah, and one from my friend Adam." He punched a few buttons. "He sent me a text. Hmm." He took a few moments to read it. "I'm not surprised at this. This one will interest you."

"What is it?" she asked.

"Adam discovered that the e-mails both you and I received originated from the Schooner Café."

"Are you saying that someone at the

Schooner Café is behind all of this?" she asked.

"No," he said, closing his cell phone. "It means that the e-mails originated from someone who happened to be using the Schooner Café's Wi-Fi. But my friend can't find who the precise person is who sent them. He's working on it, however."

"Are you going to go back to the Schooner Café, then?"

"I will, eventually, but I need to head out to the fishing shacks now."

"Can I go with you?"

He stopped and looked at her. "You want to come with me? On the snowmobile?"

"Sure," she said, surprising even herself by this boldness.

"So you've decided not to cut and run?"

"Maybe I'll cut and run later. But I'd like to know what's going on. This is about me. Maybe I could be of help. Let me just grab my jacket."

He looked down at her and did a half grin. "You're going to need more than a jacket."

"I don't have much of anything more. But I do have a wool hat and mittens. And

Nori's been so nice to me. I'm using an old pair of boots that used to belong to one of her daughters."

"Let me run up to the lodge. Maybe Nori will have something that would work."

"Boots are one thing, but Nori is miles taller than me."

"Maybe her daughters, then. Don't go anywhere."

In no time at all Alec was back with a snowmobile suit of Nori's, which fit her just about as expected. The tips of her fingers landed somewhere in the elbows of the suit and the legs of the suit dragged along the floor. Still, by rolling up the sleeves and the legs they managed to get it to fit—more or less.

Outside, he said, "If your hands get cold you can just roll down the sleeves. Here's the helmet."

She eyed him. "So you just happened to bring along an extra helmet?"

"Just in case. Have you ever been on one of these before?"

"Never. And I even grew up in Maine."

"How about a motorcycle?"

She told him she had.

"It's just like that. Sit behind me, put your arms around me and hang on."

She held on tight and soon they were speeding across the flat surface of the lake.

It was exhilarating! For a moment she decided to allow herself to forget about all the threats and murders and just concentrate on the raw beauty of God's creation. The white. The cold. The flat expanse of ice.

Twenty minutes later, Alec slowed. There was an island out in the middle of the frozen white. It was a lump of land smothered with snowy fir trees. Alec drove around the island slowly.

On the side of the island facing an open part of the ice was what looked like an inlet, or it would be in the summer. Alec slowed and pointed.

"There it is," he said.

She could only see the back of the vehicle but she could see it was a truck. It looked as if someone had driven it as far into the trees as he could before abandoning it.

Alec sped up and drove away.

"Where are we going?" she yelled.

"We have to visit with Earl. He's the one who gave me the tip about the truck."

They were approaching a little settlement of fishing shacks.

The grouping of shacks looked like an arctic refugee camp with its minuscule, multicolored buildings scattered on the ice. There were some vehicles parked out on the ice, a few dozen dogs who ran around, some snowmobiles, plus a couple of guys sitting in lawn chairs smoking and talking.

"It's a regular little town," Megan said.

"It is. I think it's more for the social life than for the fishing. Some of these guys even have flat-screen TV hookups in there. Earl does. Look at the satellite dishes."

She did so and blinked.

"It's different for me. I go out fishing to be alone. It's my time to think and meditate and pray. I'm notorious for not even bringing my cell phone," he said.

They walked toward a dark green shed with a shiny red door. "Earl's place," Alec told her. "Earl runs the only gas station in town. If you've gotten gas in Whisper Lake Crossing, then you've probably met Earl."

"I think I have," she stated.

At the red door Alec said loudly, "Knock knock."

"Come in, come in," came a deep voice from inside.

Alec opened the door and ducked into the room. Megan followed.

A smiling man, with a plaid cap and dark green jacket, was wedged with pillows into a lawn chair. He said, "Come in, have a seat. Forgive me if I don't get up. The ol' back ain't what it used to be."

"How's the back?" Alec asked.

"Fair to middlin'. Gettin' better maybe. Got another MRI coming up. Can't stand up for any length of time, but the day I have to give up fishing is the day I pack 'er in." To Megan, he said, "Fell off a roof a while ago. Did a number on my back."

"I'm sorry to hear that," she said.

"It happens. Stuff happens. It happens to the best of us."

She nodded.

Earl said, "Don't just stand there with your faces hanging out, take a seat." Alec pulled up a slatted lawn chair beside Earl.

Megan sat in a canvas chair next to him. In the center of the floor a hole was cut away in the carpet and through the ice. Deep down she could see the flatness of white cold water. Beside the cutaway was a fishing rod on a metal V-stand.

Alec said, "We came about the truck, Earl. I assume it's the one I saw on the north end of Twin Peaks Island between the trees."

Earl nodded. "That'd be the one."

"When did you first notice it?" Alec asked.

"About three days ago. When the ice melts, that thing is gonna sink. We better get someone to tow if off before then. But it's not a truck I recognized, so that's why I thought I'd give you a call."

"Thanks. I'm glad you did," said Alec. "Earl, you're here a lot. Have you seen anyone that you don't know hanging around, anyone unfamiliar?"

Megan fought the urge to say, *Anyone with black hair?*

"You mean maybe the someone who drove the truck out onto the island?"

"Yeah," Alec said. "You see anyone around here who might have left it there?"

"Did see one guy. Big guy. Mid-sixties, maybe. Had a lady with him, who had long hair with this white stripe in it. Like a skunk. Both looked like hippy refugees, if you ask me."

Megan said, "I know who they are. My neighbors at Trail's End. They've rented cabins. Brad and Vicky."

"He wore sunglasses. Dark as Hades out here and he's wearing sunglasses."

Megan nodded. "That would be him."

"What did they want?" Alec asked.

"They come around wanting to rent a snowmobile. Come asking everyone. After the man come around here that's when I noticed the truck over there. The next day, in fact."

Megan wondered how a person could see all the way to the island. And then seeming to answer her question, Earl pointed to a pair of binoculars on a small folding table. Alec was right. Earl did appear to make it his business to know everyone else's business.

They chatted for a few more minutes before they left. Alec said thoughtfully to Megan as they made their way back to the snowmobile, "Maybe it's about time I met those neighbors of yours."

"Do you think they're involved in this? How could they be? I don't even know them."

"Maybe I do," Alec said. "It hasn't escaped my attention that every time I come around, your big gray-haired neighbor makes himself scarce."

Megan thought about that. The day they were walking down from the trail, Brad and Vicky had been heading right toward them. They had veered away at the last moment. In fact, Brad had taken Vicky's arm and moved her to a quick right turn. Also, they never seemed to be around when Alec was.

Megan and Alec climbed back on the snowmobile. When they reached the island, Alec parked the snowmobile and they got off. The only sound was their boots crunching across the ice. It looked to Megan as if the driver of the truck had driven around the entire island looking for the perfect hidey-hole to drive into. He had found the perfect place. She imagined that in the summer this was a natural inlet between trees, a wonderful place for a canoe, maybe even a picnic. The casual snowmobiler wouldn't even see this truck the way it was parked behind a huge fallen tree.

Alec bent down and examined the snow-covered ground at the opening of the inlet.

"What are you looking for?" Megan asked.

"Any kind of track marks." Alec knelt and with a gloved hand touched a piece of ice. He snapped a picture of it with his cell phone.

Megan knelt. "Is that a track?"

"Maybe. I don't know. My guess is that whoever left the truck here drove away on a snowmobile. If we're lucky we can get the make and model of snowmobile by the tracks."

She looked ahead at the back end of the truck. A fine skiff of snow covered it all around. Alec snapped more pictures. He said, "If I compare the amount of snow on the truck with how much snow fell recently, I can get a pretty good indication of when this truck was left here. And yes," he said moving closer, "I think this is the truck I saw someone with a gun get into that day.

"Also, the fact that Earl doesn't know this truck says a lot. Earl knows the make and model and year of every vehicle in town. He knows when anybody gets a new car. That's why I take it seriously when he calls and tells me he's seen a suspicious truck."

Before they went up to the truck itself, Alec took more pictures. He walked carefully around it. To Megan, all it was was an abandoned old rusty pickup. The back hatch was down, and there didn't seem to be anything inside of it. Alec took pictures from every angle.

"I thought cops used digital cameras," she said.

"This new phone of mine takes better pictures than my old digital camera."

Alec got a small shovel out of the back of the snowmobile and started shoveling out the bed of the truck. The license plate had been removed. "Surprise. Surprise," he said. He turned to Megan, "Can you go over by the snowmobile for a moment?"

She looked at him. "Why?"

"I'll tell you later. Just do it, okay?" His eyes looked tired. She complied. She had reached the snowmobile when he called her. "It's okay. You can come back now."

"What was all that about?"

"No one's in the cab. I just wanted to make sure."

"Oh." She thought about that. Alec was obviously looking for bodies and there were none.

He tried the driver's side door. It creaked open all the way. "Unlocked," he said. "It looks cleaned out."

Megan leaned around him for a look. The truck had an old-fashioned bench seat covered in cracked green Naugahyde, badly ripped and split.

Alec took out a small pen flashlight and aimed it into the various crevices of the truck. They went around to the passenger side. He tried the glove compartment. It appeared to be empty. No ID. He felt around inside.

"Why would someone just leave a truck like this?" Megan asked.

"When someone feels that someone else has seen said vehicle, that might be a good reason to abandon it. Or if said vehicle has been used in the commission of a crime, it might be abandoned. The other reason is that the owner just didn't want it anymore. That happens a lot around here."

He was still feeling around the inside of the glove box when he brought something out and said, "Bingo."

"What is it?"

He brought out a little plastic battery case with snaps.

"What's that for?" she asked.

"Batteries," he said. "Rechargeable batteries. Good ones. In a battery pack." He turned it over. "We're in luck. The bar code's still here and looks fairly decipherable."

"What are batteries like that used for?"

"Lots of things. Cameras. Cell phones. GPSs. PDAs." He placed it in a clear plastic bag and put it in his pocket. "We'll soon find out."

"Doesn't Bryan use batteries like that?" she asked.

His head spun around. "What did you say?"

"Bryan used to use battery packs, didn't he?"

"Bryan?"

"For his radio-controlled stuff. Don't you

remember? Remember Bryan was always into flying those planes? I remember he had packages of batteries done up like that."

"I don't think he's into that anymore. He left all his airplanes and all that stuff in a box in my parents' basement. When he got out of prison and moved away, he didn't take it with him. But thanks for reminding me. Perhaps Bryan can give me some advice and help on this. I'll photograph it and send it to him in an e-mail. See if he has any ideas."

"Yeah," Megan said. "You do that." She didn't mean for her words to come across as acerbic, but he looked at her for several seconds before he frowned.

Neither Brad nor Vicky were around when they got back to Trail's End. Nori said the couple had rented a snowmobile and had gone for the day. Alec decided not to wait for them. He would come back.

It wasn't until long after he left for home that Megan remembered she hadn't told Alec about the picture of Lorena. She wondered if it was important.

ELEVEN

Despite what his mother wanted, Alec could find no information on Bryan's girl-friend Lorena. He was currently putting a check through on the police database, but nothing had shown up yet. He sent the e-mail address on to his friend Adam, hoping the fifteen-year-old computer whiz from church would be able to uncover something.

He looked at the time readout on his computer. He decided to call his brother. He would ask Bryan about battery packs for radio-controlled models. His mother would like it that he was asking Bryan for advice. And then he would ask about his girlfriend. Maybe he could even get an address for the elusive Lorena.

It was eight here. Which meant it was six

in New Mexico. He tried Bryan's cell phone. After four rings it went to his voice mail.

"Hey, Bryan, give me a call when you get this."

He opened up his cell phone and looked for Bryan's other phone numbers. Bryan would just be getting home from work now if he wasn't working evenings. He knew that Bryan had a landline to his apartment.

Bryan's home phone rang and rang. It didn't appear to have voice mail attached to it. After six rings Alec was about to hang out when somebody answered in a brusque voice, "Hal-lo?"

"Bryan?" It didn't sound like his brother.

"Who? Who you tryin' to get?"

"Bryan Black."

"This is a pay phone."

"Okay then, sorry." Bryan must have canceled his landline or Alec had mis-dialed it. He tried again and got the same irritated guy.

"Sorry," Alec said. "I must have written down the wrong phone number."

"Who did you say you were looking for?"

"Bryan Black."

"Bryan? You mean the Bryan who lives at one forty-two? That's his name, right?"

"Yes." That was his brother's apartment number. "What phone am I calling?"

"This is a pay phone at the end of the hall."

"But you know Bryan Black?"

"You talking about that weird guy? Guy never talks to nobody. Never even takes a shower far as the rest of us can tell. If that's the guy you're talking about."

Alec blinked. This was not good. Part of Bryan's problem was that he suffered severe depression at times. He had never understood why Bryan wanted to move so far away from his home and support system after he was released from prison. However, he told their parents that he had found the Lord and wanted to make a fresh start somewhere else. "Do you live in the same apartment building as Bryan Black?" Alec asked.

"I'm two doors down across the hall from that slob."

"Do you know him at all?"

"Nobody knows that guy well. Keeps to himself, mostly. No one comes in. Hardly no one goes out."

"He has a Bible study in his apartment, I understand."

There was a laugh at the other end of the phone. "Him? A *Bible* study? You got to be kidding."

Alec ran his hand over his face. None of this sounded very good. "Have you seen his fiancée? Has she been around? She's tall and has long blond hair."

Another laugh, then the laugh quieted. "Oh yeah, wait a minute. Somebody was saying that he was bragging about some girl he met online on one of them dating services. Forget her name though."

"Lorena." Alec frowned. Bryan had said that he met Lorena at church.

"Yeah. I think that's the name I heard. But if you ask me, I don't think he's ever even laid eyes on her in real life."

Alec shut his eyes briefly and prayed for wisdom. He sincerely hoped that Bryan was still seeing the counselor he was assigned to. He said, "Listen, man, I'm his brother. And we're concerned about him out here…"

"Brother! Oh hey. Sorry for saying the

things I did. Didn't know a guy like that even would have a family."

"Everyone has a family."

There was mumbling on the other end of the line.

Alec said, "I wonder if you could give me the name and number of your apartment superintendent."

Alec wrote the information down on a piece of paper. Maybe he needed to finally visit his little brother. Had it been four years since he'd made the trip out there? Maybe he needed to go again, and maybe it should be sooner rather than later. He even wondered about today. He could leave this case in the capable hands of Stu and Steve.

He thanked the man who'd answered the pay phone and hung up.

Alec looked through the address list on his phone and realized he didn't have a phone number for Bryan's pastor. He couldn't even remember what church Bryan went to. Would his mother know? He didn't want to phone her about this. He didn't want to worry her.

Instead, he dialed the number for Bryan's apartment superintendent.

"Yeah?"

Alec introduced himself and asked about Bryan Black.

"You're the cop brother?"

"That's right. Listen, I'm worried about him."

"You should be. He's about ready to be evicted. Hasn't paid rent in two months."

Alec sighed. This was worse than he thought. "Tell me how much he owes and I'll send you a check. Better yet, when I come out I'll pay you in full. But there is something I'd like you to do. I assume you have master keys to all the apartments? I'd like you to go into his apartment and then let me know if there's anything that strikes you as wrong. I'll wait."

"Hey, man, it's supper time here, you want me to do that now?"

"His family is worried about him. I'll wait."

"Okay then." He heard retreating footsteps. Twelve minutes later the super came back on the line. "Can't get into his apartment."

"What do you mean you can't get into his

room? I thought you had a master key to all the rooms."

"I don't know, man. It's like he's got some sort of dead bolt lock on the inside. Our tenants aren't allowed to do that, but a lot of them do it anyway."

Alec breathed out a long breath. Tenants with something to hide. "Okay, here's what I want you to do. I want you to see if you can get into his room by any means possible. I'll be flying out there tomorrow. As soon as I can get a flight."

"Okay, man."

After the phone call he went online and looked at airline ticket prices. The soonest he could get out was the day after tomorrow. February 14, Valentine's Day. He was leaving to see his brother on what would be his twentieth wedding anniversary, which was the day the weatherman said a storm was coming. He could fly out of Boston. The storm was mostly tracking north. He needed to get out there. What was happening to Bryan weighed heavily on his mind.

When they were boys, Alec and Bryan

had been the best of friends, but there was a dark side to Bryan's childhood. The times that Bryan bullied the neighbor's pet, Alec took the blame. When Bryan played with fire and matches, Alec hid the matches, hid the evidence. Why had he done that? It all had to do with his mother. Even as a child, he sensed her emotional fragility, and so Alec continually covered up to protect his mother. He had lied on the stand not to protect Bryan, but to protect his mother. She wanted two happy, healthy sons. He would hear her crying at night. He would see her worried frown. He knew she suffered headaches brought on by the challenges of Bryan.

He remembered his parents taking Bryan from psychologist to psychologist when Bryan was younger. Alec knew his mother would never admit it, but that she felt a kind of relief when her youngest son was put behind bars.

Even though it was late, Alec picked up his phone again and called Steve.

"Do you feel like listening to the blatherings of a good friend?" he asked.

"Why not? You've certainly listened to my blatherings over the years."

When Steve had arrived in Whisper Lake Crossing, he was a beaten down, ex-military Special Forces operative going through a rather bitter divorce. It was Alec who had prayed with Steve and brought him around to God. Now it was Alec with the problem. He had told Steve already about his wedding and Megan's grand-mother, but now, maybe it was time to share the whole story with his friend. Even the lie.

"Talk to me," Steve said quietly.

Alec did. When he finished his story, Steve said, "You need to tell Megan this. You need to tell Megan everything you just told me."

"But what do I do about Bryan? Do I go and see what's happening out there?"

"I can't make that decision for you. I think you need to pray about it. I think you need to pray that God will help you come to the right decision."

"I already bought my ticket."

"Tickets can be canceled."

"I haven't been out to visit him in four years. He needs my help. I think he's on a downward slope. He'll end up on the street if I don't intervene."

"And what about Megan?"

"As you can see, Steve, my life is pretty much in the toilet."

"Only you can decide whether you want to go out to New Mexico now, but I will say that I think you need to tell Megan about the perjury."

"She'll never forgive me that."

"How do you know that? She may surprise you."

"You don't understand. I chose my family—my brother—over the woman who was carrying my child. I let her go. I lied for my brother on the stand. I'm an officer of the law, of the courts. And I lied."

"You weren't a police officer, then."

"She won't forgive me."

"Still, you need to tell her. I can't advise you on whether to stay here or go to your brother but I can advise you on this—you can't keep holding on to this lie. It'll kill you, man."

"It already is."

Later, he checked his e-mail. His plane

ticket had been delivered to his e-mail address. He printed it off. *God, what do I do?*

Could he live with his secret any longer?

But by booking and printing off the plane ticket, he knew he had already made his choice. It was his family again. It was always his family.

God, what should I do?

Should he follow Steve's advice and tell Megan about his lie? But what if she didn't forgive him?

TWELVE

Sitting in her pajamas by the fire sounded good to Megan. There was so much on her mind. Because a storm was coming in another day, Steve had made sure that all the cabins had firewood. They were stacks of split logs plus great piles of kindling.

She pulled on some boots and opened the back door to her cabin, and put the kindling basket under her arm. She gasped silently and shrank back into her kitchen. There was some sort of little black animal sitting on the top of her garbage can lid and moving around.

"Ugh!" she said out loud. What she didn't need now was an encounter with a skunk. In the safety of her kitchen, she looked through her window at the animal. It was still there. But something about it looked curious. It looked as if it was bobbing its head forward and back and forward and back. What kind of an animal did that?

Out of the corner of her eye she saw a movement. Brad was over behind his own cabin, piling firewood in the cloth carrier bags provided in the cabins. He held his belly with both hands as he gathered wood.

She might think he was a little weird, but she was also quite confident that she had put her foot down about the whole *sugar* thing. Maybe he could help her scare away the skunk.

She opened her door a crack. "Brad!" she called. He looked over. "Are you busy?" she asked. "There's an animal on my garbage can. I think it's a skunk." She pointed.

"An animal? I don't see anything."

"It's still there. It won't move."

She pointed to her garbage can. It was still there moving around the lid of garbage can. But why wasn't it running away? Most animals would be scurrying away by now. Brad came toward it tentatively, a rather large piece of wood held over his head.

"Don't kill it," she said. "Just chase it away."

"I don't see anything. It's on your garbage can, you say?"

"Well, of course you can't see anything. It's dark out here. I don't see how you can see anything with sunglasses on at night."

He stopped, looking up at her. "I have an eye problem. Doctor's orders."

"Sorry."

"It's okay. I see it now. A little black thing."

"Right. Is it a skunk?"

He walked slowly, step-by-step, toward it. "Be careful," she said. "If it's a skunk you don't want to be sprayed!"

"It couldn't be a skunk. I think they hibernate in winter."

"Well, something's there."

He moved slowly toward it, his boots squeaking on the snow. The animal just kept bopping. With the end of his piece of wood he poked at the animal.

"Ew," Megan gasped, covering her mouth with both hands.

He started laughing. He held the stick

toward her. On the end of the stick was a piece of black fur. She backed away from it.

"It's not an animal," he said. "It's just a piece of fur or something. Look."

She walked down the steps. He moved the piece of wood in her direction. Cautiously she came toward the thing. It fell into her hands. She pulled away and the thing fell onto the porch. It was a wig. *A black wig.*

Megan's eyes were wide, and she could hardly breathe.

"It looks like a wig. Is it yours?" Brad asked.

"No!"

"What's the matter?"

"Nothing." She regained her composure. She didn't feel like telling Brad what was going on with her. "It just scared me, that's all," she said.

"It's not yours?"

"No. It's not mine."

He stopped, put a finger to his chin. "I think it's Vicky's. I'm fairly sure this is hers."

"Why would she have a wig like this?" Megan took it from Brad and examined it more closely. It was an adult wig of short, spiky, thick black hair. She placed the wig back down on the garbage can lid and noticed the head for the first time. A hairless doll's head with a creepy smile was bobbing up and down. Brad picked it up. "It's a bobblehead," he said. He looked at her. "Is *this* yours?"

She shook her head rapidly. "It's not mine."

Brad picked up the wig and the head. He looked at her. "You look so scared."

"Well, wouldn't you be? A black wig on top of a doll's head?"

"I admit it's weird."

"It's more than weird. It's like being in horror movie!"

He grinned. "I'm sure there's a reasonable explanation."

She asked, "What are you going to do with them?"

"I'll give the wig to Vicky the next time I see her. Maybe the head is hers, too. You know how Vicky is. I wouldn't be at all surprised if she set these up on your can. Maybe she thought it was artful or something."

Suddenly, Megan wanted to be in her

little cabin with her doors locked and her windows shut and her curtains drawn more than just about anything in the world. "I've got to go in," she said.

She picked up her basket of kindling and was about to say goodbye when she was conscious of Brad standing close behind her. "Allow me," he said, opening her door for her. "Your hands are full."

"Thank you."

But once inside, he didn't leave. He just stood there looking down at her.

He said, "I'm worried about you."

"Don't be worried about me."

"Maybe," he said. "Maybe you need someone."

"Someone?"

"Megan," he said, his voice breaking. "I was wondering something. I hope you can humor an old man. You and me." He pointed at her and then at himself. "We… uh…we seem to have a connection. I don't know if you've felt it or not. I certainly have. And I was going to ask you, if we could, if you would like to go out to dinner with me sometime. Maybe we can see each other. It would make me so very happy."

"Brad, I…" She hesitated, backing away. "I'm seeing someone right now." He thought they had a *connection?* They barely knew each other. "I thought you and Vicky were seeing each other," she blurted out.

"Ah, poor Vicky. She has her problems, and I've come to understand that she and I don't have very much in common," he said.

"But you spend so much time together."

"She'll tell you that I talk about you most of the time when I'm with her."

Megan was shocked to her core.

He continued, "Did you get all the text messages I sent to you today?"

Megan nodded, swallowing. How was she going to get rid of him?

"Brad, I…I'm sorry. But I just don't think… If I gave you the wrong impression, I'm sorry."

He folded his big hands over his big belly, cast his sunglass-covered eyes downward and said, "Forgive me, Megan. I get a little carried away sometimes. And you said you were seeing someone. I should have known, a pretty young woman like yourself. Tell me, is it the sheriff?"

Megan wanted to tell him that it was none of his business. She didn't say anything.

He continued, "I'm sorry if I offended you." He paused. "I hope you are very happy together and I hope you'll still consent to design my Web site. I live and work alone. Sometimes I don't relate to people really well. I relate more to my camera."

"It's okay."

"Do you think you can still work on my Web site?"

"I'm not so sure that's a good idea."

"But you promised." His voice had taken on an intensity that for a moment startled her. It called up something in her memory, she couldn't define it, but it filled her with a kind of horror.

Then in an instant it was gone and Brad was just Brad, a gray-haired pathetic old man who merely wanted a new Web site.

"I didn't promise," she said.

"You did. I remember." He sank down heavily into one of her kitchen chairs. Oh great. Now he would stay and stay. How was she going to get rid of him without seeming to be unkind? She remained on her feet, her arms crossed across her chest.

Eventually he got up. "I suppose I should get going," he said wearily.

She nodded. "It's late. And thanks for your help with the skunk."

"It was my pleasure," he said as he shuffled out. She watched the back of him as he padded across the snow to his cabin. She put a hand to her mouth. There was something about him which was so familiar and yet it wasn't.

In the morning, Megan called Alec. After the first ring it went to his voice mail. She left an urgent message for him to call her just as soon as possible. After ten minutes passed and he still had not returned her call, she tried again. It went again immediately to voice mail.

She paced the little cabin. Alec needed to know about the wig. Brad had taken both the wig and the bobblehead with him. She knew because she had looked out in the morning and the bobblehead was not on the trash can. What was Vicky's involvement in all this? Who was she? Those were the questions she had asked herself all night as she tossed and turned in bed.

She also really needed to talk with Alec about his brother's girlfriend. She tried calling him once more, but the call went to his voice mail. She packed up her computer, zipped up her jacket, put on her boots and grabbed her car keys. She wasn't sure she even knew where Alec lived, but she needed to see him.

She headed straight for the Schooner Café. Maybe Marlene knew where Alec lived. And if Marlene wasn't there, then someone else would tell her Alec's address, she was sure.

The waitress, whose name tag proclaimed that she was Cindy, shook her head. She was new in town and didn't know too many people. She didn't know Alec. Megan looked around helplessly.

Two wizened old men approached her. One introduced himself as Pete and the other as Peach. The one whose name was Pete was only her height and had fine, thin, white hair and blue eyes.

"We couldn't help but overhear you. You want to know where Alec lives? We can show you, Peach and I can."

The man whose name was Peach said, "He lives right on this street. Two doors away from here on the left."

"Yep." Their heads nodded. They gave her directions and she soon found Alec's house. It was an old row house with the snow neatly shoveled away on the walk. The small front porch was just feet from the road. There were lights on inside and she walked up to the house and pressed the doorbell.

Alec opened the door, a cell phone pressed into his ear. When he saw it was her, his eyes lit up and he motioned her inside. She entered and followed him down a short hall into a sitting room where they sat on mismatched chairs. Everything in his small house was like him, organized and clean and neat.

When he closed his phone, he said, "Meggie. I was just thinking about you. I need to talk to you about something…."

"Well, that makes two of us because I need to talk to you." She went on without stopping. "There was a wig on top of my garbage can last night. It was on top of one of those bobble-headed dolls—like the kind Denise has in her house…" She told him that Brad said it belonged to Vicky and that Brad took the wig and bobblehead over to Vicky's cabin. "Alec, could this be the person we're looking for? She sort of fits the physical description. If you tucked her long hair under that wig, she could be my stalker! But why? I don't even know her. I don't understand."

"Megan, slow down. A bobblehead doll? Denise reported one stolen from her house."

"Well, it ended up on my garbage can lid. Don't ask me how."

"Megan, can you go over your story once more?"

She did, slower this time, while he wrote everything down. He shook his head. "I've got to get this information to Stu right away."

"Plus, there's something else." She unzipped her computer case, pulled out her laptop and opened it to the bookmarked page. "This doesn't have anything to do with the black-wigged stalker, but I found out that Lorena doesn't exist." She explained how "Lorena" was really a manipulated model image used for art shots.

Alec studied the image. His face fell. "This is what I've been suspecting." His voice was quiet and, when he raised his head, his eyes were sad. "My brother's in trouble." He looked down at his notebook.

"I want to get this information about the wig and bobblehead to Stu. He'll be handling this for a few days. I had to make a right decision."

"A decision about what?" she asked.

"I've booked a flight for tomorrow night to see my brother."

"You're going away tomorrow?"

"I won't be gone for more than a day or two, but…"

The silence lengthened. Megan didn't know what to say. How could he even think of leaving when there was a murderer around? "But what?" she asked.

"There's something else I need to tell you."

"Go on," she said.

He began, "I've carried this secret for twenty years. I lied on the stand to protect my brother. I wasn't with him the evening your grandmother was pushed down the stairs."

"What are you saying?"

"I wasn't with my brother that day. He asked me to lie for him and I did. I lied to protect him and I have deeply regretted that every day of my life since."

Megan said, "You chose your brother over me."

He nodded. "I did."

"And you're still doing that."

"What do you mean?"

"I'm being stalked, and you're flying out tomorrow night to see your brother. What if it's your brother who's doing all this in the first place? What if Vicky is Lorena? What if she and Bryan are doing this?

"I can't believe you're doing this again, Alec. Even when we were dating, poor, troubled Bryan always came first. You are more worried about Bryan's safety than you are about mine." She shook her head. She would regret saying this later, but she had to continue. "I don't think there is a future for us. You'll always be running to your brother, bailing him out."

"That's not true. I…"

She stood up. "Your family defended Bryan, even when my grandmother said he pushed her… She told me. I have no idea why he did it, but I believe what my grandmother said." She backed toward the door. "I'm leaving. I came here because I thought you could help me with the wig. But you can't, can you? All you can do is worry about your brother. I already know he killed my grandmother. But, what if Bryan killed Sophia and Jennifer and Paul? You can't even face reality. What if Bryan is here?"

"Wait," he called after her. "What do you mean by Bryan being behind this? Have you seen him?"

There was real concern on his face. Megan hesitated but only for a second. No, she hadn't seen Bryan. But that didn't mean he wasn't behind this.

Alec's cell phone rang. He ignored it. *You better answer it. It might be your precious brother,* she thought, but didn't say. Was she selfish in thinking this way? She didn't know, but maybe she, too, should leave. Maybe she would be safer in Baltimore.

"I'm leaving, too," she called after him. "I'm driving home tonight."

"Megan! Wait! Don't leave. A storm is coming!" But she was already on her way back down the icy sidewalk to her car.

It was snowing lightly. Her wipers slapped across her windshield. If she packed up now she could be gone by nightfall. And this time she would make herself forget all about Alec. This time she wouldn't be back. But she had to hurry. The storm was on its way.

So much for honesty. Alec had finally been totally one hundred percent honest and Megan had walked out. Just like he knew she would. Just like he would if the shoe was on the other foot.

He was about to lift the phone receiver to call Bryan when his phone rang. It was his mother, finally connecting with him. He wondered if he should tell her about Lorena, or about Bryan's rent. Or about the fact that Bryan had double locked his apartment. It was good that he was flying out there. He needed to figure out what was going on. And maybe when he got back home he'd try to figure out what to do—if anything—about Megan. All of these mixed up thoughts flitted through his mind when he said hello to his mother.

"Alec, I need to talk to you about your brother. I should have when you and Megan were here, but I was afraid. Bryan is in some kind of trouble. I can just sense it."

When he told her he was going to New Mexico, his mother heaved a huge sigh of relief. "I'm glad to hear that. There's something going on that I don't understand. It's probably nothing but I can't be too sure."

"What? Have you heard something? Seen him?"

"Seen him? No. Why would you ask?"

Alec checked himself. "I don't know. Go on."

"Alec, it's funny that you would ask me that. The reason that I wanted to talk to you is that Mrs. Covington told me she saw your brother in Bangor a few weeks ago."

"That's impossible." But even as he said it, he wondered.

"Alec, she was very sure. She said she saw a man who looked exactly like Bryan."

"How would she know Bryan, twenty years later? He's never come back here at all." He sat down on the couch and cradled his forehead with his left hand.

"She said it was a man who looked, in her words, exactly like Bryan would look, only twenty years later."

Alec shook his head. "If Bryan was here, then he would've called us. He would have called me." Bryan called him all the time, usually about simple things. How could Bryan be in Maine and him not know about it? Or did he not know his brother the way he thought he did?

"She says he looked right at her, and she swears he recognized her, but turned and crossed the street. When she told me this I called the electronics store in New Mexico, and Alec, your brother hasn't been to work in several weeks."

Alec closed his eyes. Something was definitely wrong and getting worse. "Mother, why didn't you tell me this when we were visiting?"

"I tried to. I wanted to. I know I should have, but I couldn't get the words out. As soon as you and Megan left I realized that I should have, and decided I needed to call you right away."

Alec sighed.

"Did you find anything out about Lorena, like I asked?"

"Oh yes. Yes, I did."

When he told her what Megan had found, there was a strangled cry on the other end of the phone.

His voice was almost a whisper when he said, "I'll figure it out, Mother. I'll let you know what's going on."

Alec's next call was to his brother.

"Hey, bro," Bryan answered.

"Where are you?" Alec tried to remain calm, but he paced while he talked.

"In my apartment, watching the tube."

"And where would that be?"

"What do you mean where would that be? You've been to my apartment lots of times."

"So you are in New Mexico right now."

"Where else would I be?"

"Here," Alec said. "Here in Maine. One of Mom's friends saw you in Bangor."

"Me in Bangor?" Alec heard a loud

guffaw. "That'll be the day. I wouldn't go back to Maine if my life depended on it. Why would I? Everyone hates me there. Besides I got a nice girlfriend here. I go to church. We're getting married."

"And that's another thing. It's about your girlfriend. Do you know her real name is Mandy, and that she's not a real person?"

There was a long silence. Bryan's voice was quiet when he said, "Of course she's a real person. She was over here this morning as a matter of fact. Alec, you're scaring me. What's all this about?"

Alec leaned forward, putting his elbows on his knees. Could Megan have it wrong? But no, Alec had seen the picture of Mandy with his own eyes. "I'm coming for a visit, Bryan. I'll be there in twenty-four hours."

"Hey, that's great. Lorena and I will show you a great time. You'll be here in time for the Bible study."

"What about your job?"

"What about my job?" Bryan asked.

"You haven't been to work at the electronics store."

"What are you—a private detective? I quit

that minimum-wage job. Lorena and I are going into business together. I was going to tell you about this. It was a surprise. That's why she was here this morning. We're setting up a carpet cleaning company."

When Alec hung up he stood for a long time looking out the window. Either Bryan was telling the truth and Megan had figured it out all wrong, or Bryan was the smoothest liar on the planet.

Alec would know in less than twenty-four hours.

THIRTEEN

Megan didn't leave that night. She decided she didn't want to drive in the dark. Her suitcase was all packed, and if she left early in the morning, she could be in Baltimore by evening. It was much better to drive during the day in the winter.

By morning it had already begun to snow, however. Megan felt she had no recourse but to stay in her cabin, work on her Web sites and wait out the storm. It didn't escape her notice that today was Valentine's Day.

Earlier that morning she had seen Steve and Nori and their girls drive past on their way to the airport. They were going to Boston to pick up Steve's son who was coming to Trail's End for a visit. The boy lived with Steve's ex-wife. Alec had probably gone to the airport by now. Brad and Vicky were still here. She had seen Vicky the previous night gathering wood and Vicky had expressed excitement at being here during such a big storm.

"Oh, it'll be so much fun!" she had said.

"Hey, Vicky," Megan had said sidling up to her. "Did Brad give you back your wig?"

Vicky stopped. "Wig? Why would Brad be giving me a wig?"

"I found a black wig on top of my garbage can. Brad said he thought it was yours."

Vicky laughed and fingered her long hair. "With this much hair, you think I need a wig?"

"Just curious."

"Oh, that Brad. What a character he is."

But Megan didn't leave. The snow was coming. She had no choice but to wait it out. She would attempt to get some work done today.

By lunchtime the snow was swirling around her cabin windows, and by late afternoon, the blizzard was in full force. Snow had piled halfway up on her door. The windows were covered with it. Some had even come down the chimney and landed on her burning firewood.

Megan exhaled deeply and stretched her fingers, uncramping them from the hours of computer work she had just done. She had come so close to allowing herself to fall in love again. She had come so close to allowing herself to feel again. And now Alec was gone.

The knock on her door almost made her jump out of her skin. Her cabin lights went out at just about the same time. It was Brad who stood at her door. Snow fell off the brim of his hat and caught in his beard. He really did look like Santa Claus.

"Yes?" She opened the door a crack. He was all smiles.

He said, "It's just me. You look like you've seen a ghost. You okay?"

"I'm okay." She still hadn't opened her door more than six inches.

"Vicky and I were just wondering if you wanted to come over and work on a jigsaw puzzle with us. I see you lost power, too."

"I guess I did."

"My cabin has a whole shelf full of jigsaw puzzles."

"That's nice."

He reached up with one motion, grasped the door from her hand and opened it up. He walked right in past her, climbing over the drift of snow that had already accumulated on her sill. "Hope you don't mind. I just want to see your power box. Mine's all fluky. So's Vicky's. I was up at the lodge trying to get the generator going. Do you know anything about generators?"

Megan shook her head. "Nori said Steve showed you how to run the generator should the power go out."

"Steve showed me, but I couldn't get the generator running. The phone lines are out, too. It's really coming down out there. They're saying it's going to be worse than they thought."

She felt the tiniest frisson of fear go through her body like an electrical current.

She said, "But we'll all be okay. We have plenty of firewood and candles. And Steve and Nori will be back tomorrow."

"I doubt the roads will be plowed by then. It's going to take days to dig out after this.

Nope, I'm thinking the three of us are going to be on our own here for quite a while."

He was standing close to her, looking down at her and grinning. She could see his eyes through the gray lenses of his sunglasses. They seemed cold and hard despite his smile. She hugged her arms around her and moved away from him a bit. He took a step toward her. He was making her nervous.

He said, "I thought that since we're the only ones here, the three of us could hang out together."

The only ones here. "I've been spending the day working on my computer," she said. "That's what I plan to do."

"But the power's out."

"I've got five hours of battery time."

He grunted. "You can't get Wi-Fi. It's out. I tried it. That was my thought, too. Get started on my documentary."

"We can try to get the generator going. It can't be that hard."

He took off his glasses, folded them carefully and put them in the pockets of his coat. It was the first time she had seen his eyes.

She stared hard at him. They looked at

each other for a long time. She suppressed a shiver because suddenly she realized who he really was.

Did he see her shock? The silent gasp? Did he know that she knew his true identity? Her only chance was to pretend she didn't know. She glanced at the door surreptitiously.

"Brad, uh, I think I'm going to head outside and get me some more firewood." If she could get past him, she would run far away from him.

"That's not needed. You've got plenty stacked up in here. And it looks like your suitcases are packed. What do you need with so much wood when you're going home?"

She shrugged. "As you said, it might be a long time before I can think about driving home."

"And where's home for you? You never did tell us, you know."

"Plattsburgh, New York." It was the first city that came to her mind.

He chuckled.

She said, "I still need kindling, though."

"Plenty of kindling here."

She tried to laugh it off. "Not the way I make fires. I seem to need a lot. I want to stock up before it gets snowing too much."

"You don't need it." His voice was harsh. It was a command.

She moved toward the door, purposefully. "I'm getting some anyway, Brad." She had to get out. She had to get away from him.

He pushed in front of her. "No. You don't need to go anywhere."

"Brad—um…"

She backed into her kitchen looking for anything that might serve as a weapon, hoping he hadn't seen where her eyes had settled—a sharp paring knife lying in her sink. She backed toward the counter, her hands behind her. She reached for the knife, was able to grab it. In the dim light of the kitchen she was pretty sure he hadn't seen the way she'd shoved it into the pocket of her jeans.

"It'll be just the three of us tonight," he said. "You and me and Vicky. Do you like jigsaw puzzles? There's lots of jigsaw puzzles at my cabin. We could put one together. See if we can get all the puzzles pieces to fit together. Puzzles are like that. They take a lot of figuring, lots of hard thinking."

He knew she knew!

"Okay," she said, her voice light, "Let's go to Vicky's then." Megan stepped into her boots. Outside she would run.

"No. I changed my mind. We're not going to Vicky's. Don't you know what day this is?"

"No," she said, trying to keep her voice light.

"It's our wedding day."

The words hit her like a punch. It was several seconds before she found the breath to answer. "What are you talking about, Brad?"

"I've been planning our wedding for twenty years," he said. "I even put an offer on a house. You'll like it. I sent you a picture."

She stared at him. He began shedding bits of himself. The first thing to come off was the gray wig. He threw it on the kitchen table. Next was the beard, which he peeled off from right to left. He massaged his chin. "Whew, that stings," he said.

She looked on horrified as he reached in and seemed to pull out his teeth. "You can get these at any good gag store. They're professional. I got these teeth at a place that makes disguises for professional actors. Really good, aren't they? It takes a bit of practice to learn how to talk with them and eat with them. And you end up having to brush them like real teeth."

"Bryan…" Her voice was hoarse.

"The last thing is this fat suit. I'm glad that it's winter rather than summer. This thing is so hot. I don't know how professional Santas do it."

"What do you want?" The knife was in her pocket. She would use it if she had to.

"What do you mean, what do I want? What I've always wanted. What's always been mine. You left me for Alec. But I made sure your wedding never happened."

"You killed my grandmother just so the wedding wouldn't go through?"

He leaned back his head and chuckled. "How do you like my chuckle? I worked on it. My cellmate was an actor. He taught me all kinds of things."

"You went to jail for killing my grandmother."

"I know. That little part of my plan wasn't supposed to happen. But I've had twenty years to make new plans."

"You killed Sophia and Jennifer?"

"Had to. Time was running out. I didn't know where you were. You kept yourself well hidden. I figured that killing them would bring you right to my brother. And it did."

He was a madman. "What about Paul?"

"Paul was for good measure. I was on a roll."

"You're a monster!" She shrank back from him and leaned against the wall. He moved closer to her.

"I went to see your grandmother that day. I needed to persuade her to tell you that the wedding should be called off. She was the one who could do it. I told her that you were carrying my baby."

"How did you know I was pregnant?"

"That's simple. Alec told me. Alec told me everything. He still does. We are close. We're brothers." He held up the fingers of his left hand and crossed the second finger over the first.

"Your grandmother didn't believe that you were pregnant. I talked to her several times and told her I would kill her unless she managed to get you to call off the wedding. That you had my baby and you had no right to marry Alec. I told her if she didn't use her powers to call off the wedding I would kill her to get my baby."

His grin was wild and feral. She had to remain calm. She prayed that he wouldn't see the knife bulging in her pocket. Her only salvation would be to maintain her cool. He couldn't know how afraid she was.

She asked, "Who's Vicky? Is she the girl-friend you told your family about?"

"Vicky?" He looked toward the cabin door and sighed. "No, she's exactly who she says she is. She's a tourist coming here to soothe her wounds from a bad relation-ship. I have her."

"What? Where is she?"

"She'll be coming with us."

"With us where?"

"To our new house, of course. We're leaving in a few minutes. Today is our wedding day. You can't forget that, can you?"

She stared at him. "We'll never get anywhere in this blizzard."

Snow slashed against the windows like handfuls of wet sand. He lunged toward her and grabbed her wrists. He was stronger than she expected.

He said, "It's time for you to come with me now."

"No!" she screamed as loudly as she could. He merely laughed.

"No one will hear you. You, me and Vicky, we're the only ones here now. I made sure of that. I sent the e-mail to Steve and Nori about his son's flight arriving two days early. And boy did I get lucky with a storm! Even your beloved boyfriend is off taking care of his poor benighted brother."

She fought against him but he only held her tighter.

"I've finally got you and I'm not about to let you go."

"You're terrible. You're a monster. I'll never go with you. Never."

She yelled. She kicked. She screamed. But he held her tightly. She said, "You did all of it. The invitations, the e-mails, the wig, the flowers, why?"

"I've loved you from the beginning. I will be your husband and you will learn to love me like you love Alec. It won't be hard. Alec and I are brothers."

"What was the wig and doll's head all about?"

"I needed you to be afraid. I needed you to need me. And you did. You needed me to rescue you last night."

She shook her head. "You're crazy."

He let go of her hands, and cupped her cheeks in his palms. He brought her face within inches of his own. "I thought of nothing but you for twenty years. You will learn to love me." His breath was sour and she fought to move her face to the side but once again he brought it even closer. He was about to clamp his lips on top of hers when she spit in his face.

"I will never love you. Never!"

He kept the spittle on his nose and grinned at her. "I forgive you for doing that," he said. "I will forgive you every-thing. Including the abortion."

She stared at him, dumbfounded. He was insane, more insane than she realized. "I never had an abortion."

"Of course you did. You got rid of our baby. But I forgive you. I know it was my baby rather than Alec's."

She couldn't believe he was saying this. Could he be that deluded?

He continued, "I know you pretended it was Alec's baby because you were momentarily blinded into thinking you were in love with him. He did that to you, but I've known all along that it's me you really love. That's why I had to find you. That's why I've been planning this for twenty years."

Her eyes were wide. She had to get away from this madman, but how? She squirmed and he chuckled. "I love the way you playact. Pretending that you hate me, but I know the truth. I know what's in your heart."

She saw her chance. With one quick movement she reached into her jean pocket, pulled out the paring knife, thrust it forward and watched horrified as it sank into his jacket. Had she even broken his flesh?

He yelled and staggered backward, his

eyes wide and full of horror as he gazed at the knife handle sticking out of his arm. Then his demeanor suddenly changed. Smiling, he calmly pulled it out of his jacket, threw it from him and it clattered on the floor. He was bleeding a little, but he hadn't been injured badly. Probably it had just nicked his skin.

He grabbed her arms more harshly this time. "Okay," he said. "You want to play rough I can play rough. I like rough games." From his pocket he extracted a thick cable tie and bound her wrists together in front of her. She looked down helplessly at them.

She thought about Alec, who was even now on his way to take care of his little brother. How could one family produce one son who was so good and decent and another who had turned so terribly wrong? It came to her then too, that she wanted Alec. She wanted to give them another chance. She didn't want Bryan to win. She also began to realize how hard it must have been for Alec, how torn he would be most of the time. Family was family, after all.

She didn't want to die. She realized that

her only salvation might be to play along with Bryan. She said, "Hey, Bryan." She lifted her hands. "I didn't mean to hurt you with a knife. You're right. I was just playing along. But this wrist thing has gone a bit too far, don't you think?"

He chuckled. "You're not getting away from me. We're leaving now."

"I was thinking, why don't we wait out the storm here?" She glanced outside. "We'll never be able to get anywhere in this."

"You underestimate your old friend Bryan. Get on your coat."

"How can I get my coat on with my hands tied up with like this?"

He picked up the bloody paring knife from the floor and with one quick snip the ties were undone. She wanted to run, but she didn't know where Vicky was. An innocent person like Vicky shouldn't be caught up in all of this. She put on her mittens and coat and tried to come up with a plan. He was watching her carefully. There would be no grabbing of another knife. Then she remembered that her car keys were deep inside the pocket of the jacket she had just put on. She carefully zipped it up making sure they didn't jangle. She didn't know how, but they might come in useful.

The snow was already knee-deep and falling fast when they ventured outside. He pointed down at the frozen lake and laughed. "Aren't I clever?"

She couldn't believe her eyes. A big dump truck with a blade was out on the ice. Its lights were on and it was idling on the lake.

"A snowplow?" She looked at him.

"Of course. What better way to get where we're going?"

They plodded in the deep snow. "We'll drive to our new home in this."

Bath, she thought. They were on their way to Bath. All she could do was pray that Alec—or someone—would clue in.

He told her to climb up into the passenger side of the snowplow and she did so. There was some sort of shackle attached to the metal floorboard and he chained her ankles to it and locked the chain in place with a key. Then smiling, he pocketed the key in the inner pocket of his jacket. He went around and got in the driver's seat and started up the huge and powerful machine. Bryan leaned over and did up her seat belt. "Safety first," he chuckled.

He thrust the gearshift forward and they started lumbering across the lake.

She asked him, "Where's Vicky?"

"Safe." He said this without looking at her.

Safe. She looked behind her where the snowplow's tracks were being swallowed up by the snow as quickly as they were made.

Would anyone find her here? Alec was gone. Steve was gone. It was just her and a crazy man in a huge snowplow.

Alec should have left last night. Right at this moment, he should be sitting in the airport in Boston waiting for the flight to Albuquerque. But he just couldn't bring himself to leave.

He couldn't stop worrying about Megan. Yes, he'd left Stu in charge of the case. Besides, Megan was probably in Baltimore by now. But he couldn't stop thinking about her. His suitcase was packed, but he couldn't walk out that door. And the longer he left it, the worse the roads were getting to be. He bowed his head. For a long time he stayed that way. When he looked up he had made his decision.

He wouldn't go. Instead, he would work on the case. Megan was gone, but maybe it was time to meet the elusive Brad and Vicky.

Today was Valentine's Day. He didn't know why he felt such a foreboding, he just did. Both he and Megan had received wedding invitations with Happy Twentieth on them. Was there some significance to the date?

He didn't want to think about his brother, didn't want to blame the brother he had defended and protected his whole life, but his thoughts went unbidden back twenty years.

After every date Alec had with Megan, Bryan would come into his room and ask him all about it. Even late at night Bryan would go into Alec's room and ask lots of questions.

How is she? Where did you go? What did you talk about? What did you say? What did she say? Did you kiss her? At that point Alec would answer lightly, "And that, bro, is where my answers stop."

Then there would be good-natured

tussling between the two of them, lots of laughter. Bryan always ended up playfully punching Alec's shoulder and saying, "The best man won."

Could it be that Alec mistook all of Bryan's questions not as brotherly interest in Alec, but interest in Megan herself?

Alec ran a hand over his face and looked out at the blizzard. He called Megan on her cell phone. But a recorded message said that the lines were not operating. What lines? Megan should be home in Baltimore by now. He couldn't even leave a message. He checked her business card. He didn't even have her home number, just her cell phone number and e-mail.

He called the forensics lab in Augusta, where he had shipped the battery pack to be checked for fingerprints, to ask if there had been any headway made on the battery bar code.

"We just got that in. Turns out it's from a hobby shop in New Mexico. Las Cruces, New Mexico."

When Alec hung the phone up he knew how wrong he'd been about Bryan. Megan was right. Bryan was obviously responsible for all that happened. Maybe Bryan was holing up in one of the cabins at Trail's End even now. Steve said he had checked them yesterday and had found nothing, but if Bryan was smart enough to carry out this plan, he was smart enough to stay hidden.

Alec needed to get out to Trail's End. He hoped Megan was home by now, but there were two other guests out there who might be in danger.

The wind was coming in with a fury and snow had already drifted against his door. He wondered how much time he had before his four-wheel drive would not make it down the road at all. He grabbed his gun, his flashlight, his radio. He dressed in layers and layers of warm fleece and went outside. He swept off his car in the wind, started it and prayed that he wasn't too late.

His car fishtailed dangerously, but he managed to keep it on the snow-covered streets. His was the only vehicle on the road. All the smart people had heard the weather forecast and the police warnings urging people to stay home and inside tonight. His only luck would be that Bryan wouldn't be able to get anywhere either.

He headed down the road that led to the Trail's End turnoff.

He steered right. Then left. He tapped the brakes. Still nothing. So far he wasn't panicking. He'd taken enough winter defensive driving courses that he knew how to get out of a skid on an icy road. And yet, when he tapped on his brakes ever so slightly, the way he'd been taught, nothing was happening. He tried again. Awareness dawned on him. His brakes were gone. By the time he figured this out, he was careening sideways down the road. Ahead of him was an embankment that led down to the lake. It was coming quickly, too quickly. He felt in those seconds what Paul must've felt as his car sped over the cliff, or what Sophia or Jennifer felt.

He gripped the steering wheel so tightly that his hands spasmed.

Megan, he thought wildly, *I've made such a mess of things.* And then going an awful speed, his car hit the snowbank.

FOURTEEN

Bryan managed to maneuver the huge and awkward snowplow across the lake. He skirted around the fishing shacks and drove up the road used by the cars and the trucks to access the fishing sheds.

"I know all the back roads to Bath," he bragged.

"How did you know I lived in Bath?" She glared at him.

"I make it my business to know everything about you. Actually," he said after a pause, "your grandmother told me."

"She wouldn't."

"She did. We were great pals. She liked me, as a matter of fact. At first."

"You fooled her."

"I fooled a lot of people. Do you know I

even go to church? They think I'm some sort
of Christian down there. Good thing I know
all the lingo. But that was all part of my plan.
I've been working on perfecting my plan for
twenty years. Alec took you away from me
once, and he won't get away with that again.
I made sure of that. I made it so he is flying
down to New Mexico." He laughed.

Megan turned away from him. He was a
monster. All she could do was stare out of
her window and pray. She prayed that God
would make her brave. She prayed that God
would make her strong. She prayed that
Vicky was okay. Her prayers seemed to be
working, because even though the storm
was all around her, even though she had no
idea where she was, or even if she would
get out of this alive, she was beginning
to feel a kind of peace that could only
come from God. She knew that whatever
happened, God loved her. God had always
loved her. God had grieved with her when
she was five and her parents died. He had
sorrowed with her when her grandmother
died and her wedding was canceled. He had
been right beside her when Jack died, and

the rest of her life loomed dark as a tunnel in front of her. He was never punishing, just loving. She looked back at her captor, and realized that he could never hurt her.

The blade in front was down and it looked like he was planning on plowing all the back roads to Bath. There were few cars on the road on this treacherous evening, which was probably a good thing. The truck bumped and lurched on. Bryan raised the blade a bit and they picked up speed.

About an hour later, he pulled alongside a gas station. "I'm getting pretty good at this snowplow business," he said. "I thought all these gears and gizmos would be hard to manage, but it's not. I should get me a job doing this. I wonder how much they pay."

Megan didn't say anything. Her ankles hurt from the chains and she was shivering. The window on her side was iced up but Bryan's side was clear. He must have blocked her defroster so she couldn't see out.

He opened up the door and snow blew in on top of her. "I'm gonna go get us some coffee and food. The mother of my children needs to keep her strength up."

Megan watched him go into the gas station. She tried banging on the window, but there was no one around. She prayed that someone would come outside, that someone would see her. She prayed for Vicky. She prayed for Alec.

"God," she breathed. "Show me what to do."

"Megan?" She heard a quiet voice from the back.

Megan turned around, as much as her shackled legs would allow.

"Vicky? Is that you?"

"I'm on the floor in the back. Brad chained me here. He covered me with a blanket and tied a scarf around my mouth. I managed to work the scarf loose, but I'm so cold I can't even feel my fingers."

"Vicky! I can't believe you're there!"

"I am. Boy, I've heard about having bad luck with men, but this takes the cake. And I'm freezing."

"There's some heat coming in at my feet. See if you can move the blanket a bit and you may feel it."

Megan heard movement from the back. "Got it. Great. This is much better."

"He isn't who he says he is."

"That's an understatement if there ever was one. He doesn't even look the same. You know him?"

"His name is Bryan Black."

"Who is he?"

"Old boyfriend."

"Well, I guess you can pick them too, huh?"

"All of what he wore was a disguise, including those funny teeth."

A groan from the back. "Megan, can you drive this thing? Can you get us out of here?"

"My ankles are chained to the floor. My keys are in my pocket and on my key ring is my little penknife. But a lot of good that will do against this chain. I haven't even tried."

Bryan was emerging from the truck stop. He held a tray with two coffees and a bag of food. "Shh. He's coming back. I'll pretend I don't know you're there."

"Good. We'll think of something."

"If you know how to pray, pray."

Bryan was climbing up onto the snowplow, a big grin on his face. "Hey sugar, I got you a coffee. But I can't remember how you take it. I guess that will be one of the things we'll be learning about each other, how we take our coffee, what foods we like. It's going to be so much fun getting to know each other."

Sugar? Megan felt like screaming, but forced herself to remain calm. Her best hope lay in playing along with this madman.

"Thanks, Bryan. So you bought us a house? Tell me about it."

"You'll love it, sugar. It's got a big yard with plenty of spare bedrooms for our big family. I want a big family, don't you? I grew up with only one brother, and he wasn't much of one, was he? He ended up stealing my girlfriend. I always felt like I was cheated, you know? I always vowed that we would have a big family, don't you agree?"

"Sure." She thought hard. "Before we head down to Bath, I have a bit of a problem, Bryan. I have to use the ladies' room."

He studied her. "The restroom, huh?"

She shrugged and tried to look as contrite as she could.

He came around and opened her door and got his keys to unlock the chains. He said, "I'll walk you in. There's only one bathroom so I'll wait right outside the door. Any funny business and Vicky will die."

"Bryan," she said, and pouted. "There won't be any funny business. We're getting married, aren't we?"

"And don't try anything funny in there. When you come out I'm going to go in and look the room all over just to make sure you haven't written on the walls or anything."

Once inside the washroom Megan stood in front of the mirror trembling, and she couldn't stop the tears from falling.

Oh God, she prayed, *I know You're in control. Please help me think of something. Anything.* She pulled down a piece of paper towel to dry her eyes.

Alec should have known that Bryan would tamper with his brakes. It was Bryan's battery pack they had found. But in his position as protector/elder brother, he made himself not see it. He had no doubt that Bryan could kill. He had killed before.

He had killed Megan's sweet grandmother, plus three of their friends. Their friends! How and why he did this, Alec didn't know.

Anyone who had killed three people would want Alec out of the way, too. Fortunately, the snowbank and the lack of other drivers on the road saved him and everyone else from serious harm. He pushed away the inflated air bag. He checked himself for injuries, but he seemed to be in one piece. The next thing was to find his flashlight and phone. He found his cell phone on the floor and called Stu with the particulars and asked him to come with his snowmobile.

He reached around for his flashlight, and found it on the floor of the passenger seat. He picked it up and at the same time his fingers touched a piece of paper. He picked it up. It was a plain white envelope with his name on it.

What was this?

He opened it up and extracted the small note card. In the same block capital letters that were written on the invitation was written: THE BEST MAN WON

The best man won.

Suddenly its meaning became very clear. Bryan was to have been his best man. It was Bryan. It was like a stab, one more jab. His mother's friend had been right. Bryan had been here, was still here.

When Stu arrived, Alec filled him in. Stu had brought along a second snowmobile helmet. Alec hopped on the back of the snowmobile. The two of them took off down the road to Trail's End.

"Something came into the department," Stu shouted to him over the storm. "Earl reported a stolen snowplow."

"Who would steal a snowplow?"

"I told him we'd get to it later. Maybe Pete or Peach did. For fun. You know those old guys."

"Crazy town."

Stu drove the snowmobile expertly down the road, even though at times it was difficult to see where he was going. Darkness was descending, which would make their search even more difficult.

All of the cabin lights were out when they got there—even the outdoor lights—and Alec suspected a power outage. But that didn't make sense. This place was on the town grid and they still had power in town.

Stu pointed at a telephone pole. Through the snow they could see that the wires had been neatly snipped and were dangling in the wind.

"They've been cut," Alec said.

Closer they saw that Megan's car was there. She hadn't driven to Baltimore. His fear increased.

He saw no lights from the cabins, no candles in the windows, no flashlights. They went first to Megan's cabin. All was darkness inside.

"Megan," he called. "Megan!"

They shone their lights around and Alec saw the wig and the beard inside the cabin. He was puzzled until he remembered the description of Brad—gray hair, gray beard, funny teeth. His light soon found a pair of white gag teeth on the table, along with a pair of sunglasses. Bryan had disguised himself. No wonder he had made himself scarce when Alec came around.

Stu was holding up a lined vest. "What's

this? Looks like a jacket with a bunch of pillows in it."

"A fat suit," Alec said without emotion. "My brother dressed himself up in a fat suit." They put all of the things they could find, including a small paring knife tipped with blood, into plastic evidence bags. Stu shone his light on two packed suitcases standing by the door.

He said, "Looks like she was planning to leave."

"But got stopped," Alec said. His fear was turning into full-fledged dread. She had to be alive. She just had to be. He loved her!

They checked the other cabins. All were devoid of inhabitants. In the cabin closest to Megan's was a lot of women's clothing and a few paperback books.

"Didn't Megan say Brad had a friend named Vicky? This is probably where she's staying."

They quickly looked through these things and then went on to the next cabin.

They spent more time in the cabin two doors down from Megan. It contained a lot of camera gear and two laptop computers.

Alec said, "I think this is where Bryan stayed. We'll have to take these computers with us."

Stu said, "There are no saddlebags on the snowmobile. We'll take as much as we can and then come back later."

"Right now the most important thing is to find Megan. Earl said that Brad came around looking for a snowmobile."

"One problem with that is that you can't fit three people on a snowmobile."

Alec thought about that. He didn't want to think the worst, but if Bryan had killed four people, it would be nothing for him to get Vicky out of the way before he took Megan. Unless Vicky was in on it.

Alec said, "We could spend all day looking through the snow for a body, however I think we have to look for Megan and Bryan. I'm pretty sure she's alive and I'm pretty sure he's got her."

"You sound sure of that," Stu said.

"He's been obsessed with Megan forever. I didn't see it. He used me to get to her." *Bath,* he thought suddenly. "He's taking her to Bath. That's where we have to go."

Stu said, "The highways are closed. I

don't think we'll get through, even with this trusty snowmobile of mine."

"We have to try." Alec felt desperate.

"If they're on a snowmobile, they won't get far. In fact, I would say we'd better get back to town or we won't be able to see the road ourselves."

Alec hopped on the back of Stu's snowmobile, and away they went. The storm was increasing. And Megan was out there somewhere in the middle of it with a madman.

FIFTEEN

The snowplow was a huge thing. This machine wasn't just a pickup truck with a blade out front. It was a full-size highway model, all metal, loud and clanky, with orange stripes and all kinds of hazard lights. Several times they passed drivers who gave them the thumbs up. Megan tried making faces, mouthing the word "help", or frowning in an exaggerated sort of manner, but no one paid attention to her, or maybe they couldn't see her through her frosty window.

Up ahead a car was down in the ditch, its four-way flashers on.

"An accident, Bryan. We need to stop and help out."

He laughed. "Yeah right. I don't quite trust you yet, Megan. You haven't proven yourself. I lost a lot of trust when you had the abortion, when you killed our baby. It will take a long time to build up that kind of trust again."

"Bryan," she argued. "You're in a snowplow. We need to stop and help out. I know you're basically a good person. I know deep down you don't want to do this. Let's stop. There could be children in that car."

"And why would you suddenly care about children when you deliberately killed ours?"

Megan knew it was no use arguing. For twenty years Bryan had deluded himself into thinking that the baby she'd carried was his and that she had had an abortion.

He slowed down, but she could see that his intention was to drive right past. A man was standing in the middle of the road waving a flashlight at them in the blowing snow.

Bryan said, "Watch me. This big snowplow can go right through people."

Megan's heart leapt in her throat. Her hands were folded on her lap. She could feel her fingernails in her skin.

The man frantically waved.

"Hang on," he yelled. "Here we go!"

He picked up speed and she screamed. At the last minute, the man jumped out of the path of the plow. Her captor merely smirked and continued on down the road. He went even faster, laughing a maniacal laugh. Megan couldn't see a thing through her window as the road snaked through the Maine woods.

The road turned abruptly, but their snowplow didn't. The blade clipped a guardrail and it zigzagged down a steep bank.

Megan gasped. Ahead of them was a frozen lake.

They hit trees and the plow almost toppled. Vicky screamed while the plow bounced all over the place. The passenger door came off as they bulldozed their way between two huge pines. Megan's legs were still shackled to the bottom of the truck, but she nearly fell out. A pine branch the size of a small log exploded through the windshield and the snowplow came to a sudden stop. Then toppled onto its side.

* * *

Halfway up the road from Trail's End, Alec yelled to Stu, "Have to bring the Staties in on this."

Stu nodded. "Maybe even the FBI. We're clearly dealing with a kidnapping situation, and he may be across state lines."

Getting the snowmobile back to the main road was tricky. It seemed as if it had snowed a foot since they had come this way. But soon they were heading down the snow-blown street to the police station in Whisper Lake Crossing. There were several calls waiting for Alec from the state patrol when he got there.

There was a curious message for him. And even now the police had sent out an APB for, of all things, a snowplow. One of the employees of a gas station had gone into the restroom and when she washed her hands she pulled down the next piece of paper towel to dry her hands, there was a message written on it in ink: *This is not a joke. My name is Megan Brooks. My friend Vicky is with me. We're being kidnapped by someone driving a snowplow. We're on our* *way to Bath, Maine. Please call Whisper Lake Crossing Sheriff Alec Black...*and his number was listed there.

The state patrol told Alec, "We don't know what it's all about, but we're taking it very seriously. But even our four-wheel vehicles are having trouble in this weather. And it's only going to get worse."

Before they hung up, the state patrol promised to keep them informed. Even so, he was beginning to feel helpless.

Stu looked out the window, "Can't we get a chopper?"

"Not in this," Alec said, but then he brightened. "But what we can do is to fight fire with fire."

They hopped on Stu's snowmobile and headed over to Earl's to borrow his pride and joy, a humongous army surplus truck. The back roads to Bath? Earl was helpful. He was familiar with the gas station where Megan had been. The three of them poured over an Atlas of Maine back roads. Earl not only loaned them his Renault Sherpa six-by-six, he loaned them a driver, Jay Forrester, who plowed for the town of

Whisper Lake Crossing and worked as a first aid ski patroller.

They loaded up the truck with a high-powered flashlight and first aid supplies, and set out on a road that didn't even look like a road anymore. Alec, Stu and Jay kept in constant contact with headquarters. Half an hour out, they got a report of a car in the ditch. A man said he had tried to flag down a snowplow but the driver must not have seen him. He was pretty shaken, he said, because he came really close to being hit.

Jay said, "Snowplowers would stop. I would. Especially on a back road. That's our guy."

Yet two hours later they had not come across the errant snowplow and its hostages. And the back roads to Bath? There were so many of them that it was like looking for a needle in a haystack. Jay driving, they eventually found the gas station where Megan had written the note. It was closed down because of the storm now, but since the owner lived across the street they were able to get the particulars. The man he described getting coffee had been Bryan! There was no doubting this or Megan's description. Alec punched his fist into his hand. She had been right here!

The three of them took off in the direction that the proprietor had pointed. They passed the place where the car had gone into the ditch. They drove slowly, carefully looking for anything that was out of order. But the snow which showed no signs of abating was covering up tracks, even the huge tracks of a snowplow, almost as quickly as they were made.

It was Jay who saw the break in the cement guardrail. He stopped and the three got out to have a better look. The break in the guardrail looked comparatively recent and ahead, down the embankment, were a few broken trees.

"Do you think they went down there?" Alec asked. "It would be pretty stupid if they did."

Jay said, "He might have lost control. Even snowplows have their limits."

They shone their high-powered spotlights down the embankment. Even with blizzard conditions they saw at the bottom what looked like an overturned snowplow.

"There it is," Stu said.

But it looked too dark to Alec. There were no lights. And it was too quiet. The three set off down the hill. Jay pulled a toboggan full of medical supplies and blankets and they trudged down the cold, dark and slippery hill.

When Stu found the broken snowplow door, Alec's heart fell even further. He raced on ahead as fast as he dared through the snow which was thigh-high in places.

"Megan!" He called as he got closer. "Megan!"

Alec shone the spotlight on the plow. The snowplow was lying on the driver's side and there were blood spatters. It looked to him like a lot of blood.

"They're not here." Jay yelled to be heard over the storm.

"But they've been here," shouted Alec.

"Look that way," Stu pointed with his flashlight. Below them was a lake and along the shore were a few fishing shacks barely visible through the blackness of the storm.

Alec called, "Let's go out there."

The embankment grew steeper next to the lake. As they climbed down the snowy, rocky slope, he saw Stu point out more blood. He prayed that it didn't belong to Megan.

On the frozen lake the walking was a bit easier, but several times they bent down to examine blood. At one point it looked like a lot of blood. They also saw drag marks. There was no doubt in his mind that Bryan had taken Megan out here. They all kept calling, and Alec wished he had brought a police bullhorn with him.

His voice was practically hoarse from calling her name. As they drew beside the first shack, Jack thought he heard a faint mewling coming from inside.

"They're here," he mouthed to Jay and Stu. No light emanated from the cabin but he could hear crying.

His gun unholstered, he made his way to the door of the fishing shack and with one quick motion he flung it open and shone his light all around inside.

"Alec!" It was Megan's voice. "You're here!"

He rushed toward her. "I'm here. Are you okay, Megan?"

"I'm okay, but Vicky's not. And be careful. He's got a gun. But he's hurt."

Alec shone his light on the scene in front of him. Bryan was on the floor holding his leg with one hand and with the other hand he had a gun aimed at Megan. Next to her Vicky was lying on the floor and all he could make out about her was a lot of hair.

"Careful, bro." The gun was aimed at him now. "I wouldn't come too close if I were you."

Bryan's skin was a pasty white, his lips were dark and he shivered uncontrollably. His left leg was on the floor but it was bent at an odd angle and around it was a pool of dark blood. Alec wondered if all the blood was coming from a fractured thigh bone. Alec knew that if Bryan didn't get help soon, he could bleed out.

"Bryan," Alec said. "Your leg. You're going to need help for your leg."

Alec came toward him, but Bryan yelled, "Stay back!" His eyes were wild. "You always took everything from me and you're not going to this time. Megan is mine! We're going to get married and you can't stop us. Not this time." A spittle of blood snaked from Bryan's mouth and Alec wondered if his injuries were internal, as well. Jay was in the room now with the toboggan full of medical supplies. He unloaded a couple of blankets and handed them to Megan. Megan laid one gently on top of Vicky.

Jay said, "Bryan, we have to get you three out of here or you're not going to be able to get married to anybody. You're bleeding pretty badly."

But Bryan faced Alec when he said, "How can you help me? You've never helped me before. All you ever did was take from me."

"I'm your brother," Alec said. "I would have given my life for you."

"You never gave me anything. Nothing."

Bryan leaned back his head and laughed, then ended up choking on his own blood. Alec tried not to think of the fact that this was his brother, his flesh and blood and that he was lying here dying on a cabin floor.

Bryan hadn't seen Stu enter and sidle

around to the back of the cabin, his gun in his hand and trained on Bryan.

Alec couldn't let Megan down. Not again.

"Bryan, I've always loved you. You are my brother. I loved you when we were growing up together, and I love you now. I want you to know that."

"No!" screamed Bryan in a voice that Alec didn't even recognize. While Bryan was screaming and lunging, Stu saw his chance. He rushed forward and grabbed the gun from Bryan's hands and quickly handcuffed them behind his back.

Megan flew into Alec's arms. He held her tightly, nestling her head into his shoulder, stroking her hair.

She was crying. "It was Bryan. All along, it was Bryan. He was pretending to be Brad. I'm so glad you stayed, that you didn't fly to New Mexico."

"I am so sorry," Alec said. "Will you ever forgive me? I never should have even thought about going away with you in so much danger."

"It's okay. It's okay. I'm just glad you're here and that you stayed. And I love you for loving your brother so much. I never had a brother. I don't know what those ties are. I shouldn't have judged you."

Alec held her tightly. She was so cold. He said, "Your note on the piece of paper towel was a very smart and brave thing to do."

She began crying again. "Bryan said he was going to come in and check all the walls. But I had my keys with me and this little penknife attached to my key ring has this tiny pen in it. So I wrote on a piece of paper towel and then I stuffed it back up in the dispenser. It was the only thing I could think of. I prayed someone would use it."

"Someone did," he said. He held her tightly. She was so resourceful and brave and beautiful and, most of all, forgiving. "You were right, Megan," he said. "You were right about Bryan and I was wrong. I've been wrong about so much."

"What I was wrong about was God. I thought I was never good enough. I thought He was always punishing me, but I learned something tonight. I learned that He loves me no matter what. I learned a little about grace."

Alec just held her and cried tears of relief.

He said, "But there's one thing I haven't been wrong about and that's how much I love you."

"I love you, too."

While the two talked, Jay and Stu were busy with Bryan and Vicky. Bryan was quiet now, and was shivering so much that his limbs actually twitched. His face looked too white. Jay was able to get a tourniquet tied to his upper thigh, but he frowned, and told Alec that he thought Bryan had internal injuries. An unconscious Bryan was lashed into the toboggan. Vicky was suffering from hypothermia and was sitting up now, conscious and wrapped in a space blanket. She would be okay. And so would Megan. And so would they.

EPILOGUE

Alec's family buried Bryan a week later. His injuries were too severe and by the time they were able to get him to a hospital, he had lost too much blood. Alec sat with Bryan on the backseat of the snowplow and talked to him all the way into town. He told him that he loved him, that his mother and father loved him. That God loved him. He didn't know if Bryan heard or not, he could only pray that somewhere deep in his unconscious that he did and that he knew. Alec took care of his brother's affairs for the very last time. Disposing of his electronics, cameras and gear came within dollars of paying off all of the debts and unpaid rent that Bryan had accumulated.

Megan went back to Baltimore after the funeral, but it was a very short trip. Within two weeks she had given her notice, called a moving company and was on her way back to Whisper Lake, driving along behind the moving van. She never thought that the moving van would make it down the little road to Trail's End, but it did.

What a fitting name, Trail's End. The cottage Peace was winterized but not furnished so she rented it for her possessions and moved back into Grace for the six weeks it took to make the wedding arrangements. Tears came to her eyes when she realized that living in Grace was even better than having her things in Peace. God had given her back Alec and, most of all, had taken her back, as well. He had been there all the time, she thought. She just had to figure out what Grace was all about.

They were married the last day of March. They had waited long enough. They had made too many mistakes already.

Their wedding was attended by Steve and Nori and their two girls, Daphne and Rachel. Steve was Alec's best man. By that time Steve's son was back home in Florida with his mother.

Marlene came with her husband, Roy, her daughter, Selena, and all the waitresses at the Schooner Café. Earl was there with his son. Denise came. Eunice flew up from Baltimore and stood up for Megan. Alec's parents were there too, happy for their son, even though they had buried their youngest the previous month.

Vicky was there. Her arm was just out of a cast. The cuts and scrapes on her face were healing nicely. She told everyone that she was moving to Whisper Lake Crossing later in the spring. She was going to live by the lake, plant a garden and write poetry.

Megan and Alec were married in the little white church in Whisper Lake Crossing. A small reception was held in the lodge at Trail's End. Much to Megan's surprise and delight, the assorted sandwiches were served on the lost antique china. Her godmother, Eunice, had kept them all these years.

"I always thought something might work out between you and Alec," she said with a twinkle in her eye.

It wasn't until a month after their wedding that the ice fully melted. Alec told her when it finally gave way it could sound like a cannon going off. The townspeople always had a big party the weekend after the ice broke up.

The third week in April, Megan was at home in Alec's house working on a Web site when Alec came in the door, holding a bouquet of red roses. She got up, as she always did when he came home, and went into his arms.

"For you," he said.

"The ice broke up this morning," she said, smiling. "I heard it."

"Yes it did. Springtime, a new beginning each year."

"And Alec," she said, tears running down her cheeks, "what a perfect person with whom to start this new beginning."

Holding her close, between kisses he whispered, "I love you, Megan."

"I love you, too, Alec." And it was true. On this early April morning, with her husband standing there with a bouquet of roses and smiling, she felt that life couldn't get any better. She felt loved and, most of all, forgiven. Whisper Lake Crossing was a special place. She loved being a part of the little church that Alec went to. She loved the lake and the ice and the people who made her feel so at home.

Yes, life was truly good for her.

* * * * *

Dear Reader,

I've always been fascinated by "first love" stories. You know the kind—where couples long separated by years and distance finally find each other. There is something about those stories that melt a place deep inside of me. I'll read them over and over. Megan and Alec's love story in *On Thin Ice* is like that. They were to be married. The wedding was all arranged. The invitations were sent and the dress was bought. But when Megan's grandmother was murdered, everything fell apart and the wedding never happened.

On Thin Ice begins exactly twenty years later and the two have "found" each other again, but the circumstances are different. Someone is threatening them. Friends have been murdered. Before they can fall in love again they have to work through their feelings, the threats against them, murders, and their understanding about God.

On Thin Ice is the second in my Whisper Lake series of books, stories set on the shores of the fictional Whisper Lake, Maine.

I hope you enjoy it. If you have a story of "first love" please send it along. I would love to hear about it. I can be reached at: Linda@writerhall.com.

Linda Hall

QUESTIONS FOR DISCUSSION

1. Alec and Megan's story is one of first love. Do you remember your first love? What do you remember about it?

2. Throughout her life Megan experienced many losses. As a result, she believed God no longer loved her. Have you experienced loss? Did you feel that God had abandoned you, even for a moment? What did you do about it?

3. Because Megan became pregnant before she was married, she felt that her losses were God's punishment for this act. Do you think this is the way God works?

4. After her grandmother's murder, Megan was so distraught that she left. What would you have done had you been in her shoes?

5. Alec was torn between his love for Megan and his love for his family.

Have you ever been torn between two opposing but important factors? How did you handle it?

6. For twenty years Alec kept a "secret sin" inside of himself. He felt that God could forgive everything about him except for this one thing. Is there something that you hold in a secret place in your soul that you feel God can't forgive? What did Alec learn about God's forgiveness? What can you learn?

7. Dorothy, Alec's mother, wanted both of her sons to be perfect, yet life has a way of not working out at times. Do you have children or family members who have not "turned out" the way you wanted or prayed for? What can you do about this?

8. What character did you identify with most and why?

9. Vicky came to Whisper Lake to get over a relationship gone bad. Right away she

finds Brad and clings to him, which later proves to be her undoing. Should she have been more cautious? Why do you think Vicky was so drawn to Brad?

10. At the very end, Alec has a choice: stay with Megan or visit his brother. In your opinion, did he make the right choice?

11. Megan lives in the cabin named "Grace." What did Megan learn about Grace and Peace by the end of the book?

One step into the living room and she froze again, pan aloft.

A hulking shape stood in shadow just inside the French doors leading out to the garden veranda. This was not Popbottle Jones. This was a big, bulky, dangerous-looking man. She raised the pan higher.

"What do you want?"

"Annie?" He stepped into the light.

All the blood drained from Annie's face. Her mouth went dry as saltines. "Sloan Hawkins?"

The man removed a pair of silver aviator

sunglasses and hung them on the neck of his black rock-and-roll T-shirt. He'd rolled the sleeves up, baring muscular biceps. A pair of eyes too blue to define narrowed, looking her over as though he were a wolf and she a bunny rabbit.

Annie suppressed an annoying shiver.

It was Sloan, all right, though older and with more muscle. His nearly black hair was shorter now—no more bad-boy curl over the forehead—but bad boy screamed off him in waves just the same. He was devastatingly handsome, in a tough, rugged, manly kind of way. The years had been kind to Sloan Hawkins.

She really wanted to hate him, but she'd already wasted too much emotion on this outlaw. With God's help she'd learned to forgive. But she wasn't about to forget.

* * * * *

*Will Sloan and Annie's faith be strong
enough to see them through
the pain of the past and allow them to
open their hearts to a possible future?
Find out in THE WEDDING GARDEN
by Linda Goodnight,
available May 2010 from Love Inspired.*

INSPIRATIONAL HISTORICAL ROMANCE

Engaging stories of romance,
adventure and faith,
these novels are set in
various historical periods
from biblical times
to World War II.

NOW AVAILABLE!

Steeple
Hill®

For exciting stories that reflect traditional values,
visit:
www.SteepleHill.com